Praise for *Shadow is a Colour (as Light is)*

'A dazzling journey through grief, love, passion and dependency,
with human frailty at its centre... I adored it!'
Celia Anderson, author of *59 Memory Lane*

'Running through is a clear passion for art and an insightful understanding
of the human heart, and what it desires. 'Shadow is a Colour as Light is' is
a truly beautiful read and, as with the best of books, I felt grateful to have
spent time in its richly realised world.'
The Big Issue

'Its exploration of how art moves us - how it speaks to our fears,
our failings, our fantasies - is one that everyone should read.'
Joe Heap, author of *The Rules of Seeing*

'As detailed and beautiful as a Cézanne painting, this is a rich
and complex story of family, love and grief.'
Annie Lyons, author of *The Happiness List*

'I cannot recommend this exquisite book highly enough...Michael's
writing is every bit as beautiful and moving as the Cezanne paintings that
inspired his story. His book is a skilful and moving exploration of how
art touches people's lives. An absolute treasure!'
Ruth Hogan, author of *The Keeper of Lost Things*

Shadow is a Colour
(as Light is)

Michael Langan

LUME BOOKS

LUME BOOKS

Published in 2020 by Lume Books
30 Great Guildford Street,
Borough, SE1 0HS

ISBN 978-1-83901-281-5

Typeset using Atomik ePublisher from Easypress Technologies

www.lumebooks.co.uk

For my mum and dad,

Irene Eleanor Langan
(18/12/1939 — 23/12/2000)
&
Thomas Langan
(19/07/1940 — 23/07/2012)

Table of Contents

Walter, Hong Kong — 2013

Walter Yeung, founder and Chief Executive of CantoCorp, stands in the burnished copper cubicle that conveys him from his private basement suite to the spectacular penthouse at the top of his headquarters. Walter uses the thirty-two seconds this elevator ride takes to tighten and adjust his raw silk, oyster-coloured necktie, unbutton and re-button his navy blue suit jacket and run a comb through the thick whorl of gunmetal grey hair that, given his age — sixty-five today — he is inordinately proud of.

CantoCorp's headquarters, as designed and built to Walter's specifications, is the apogee of late twentieth century architecture. Its main fabric is glass and the steel frame — manufactured and built by CantoCorp's own engineering geniuses — is of such delicacy, utilises the most advanced structural technology, that, when combined with the complex intersections of the facade's surfaces, renders the building virtually invisible. Many of those who come to the waterfront especially to see it will look around and above them in bewilderment before a slight shift in the angle of the sky becomes apparent, the architects' special effect is revealed, and their eyes adjust to the aerial mirage that coalesces before them. There are some who doubt the building's existence and say its proposition is so impossible — *'a crystal skyscraper!'* — it must be an outlandish hoax, that those who claim to have seen it are merely the suggestible victims of a collective hysteria. It's the kind of playful manipulation Walter Yeung relishes.

The famous penthouse suite provides its occupants with an uninterrupted, three hundred and sixty degree panorama of the city. On one side are the dark green hills above Victoria harbour that contribute to making Hong Kong's backdrop so astonishing. Individual buildings, the homes of the superrich, emerge from the trees like organic growths, as natural as the system that generates the money to construct them. The structures coalesce then into apartment blocks and high-rise offices, which, in turn, reach a critical mass as landscape becomes cityscape and tumbles to the waterfront.

In the past, some Hong Kong pressure (so squeezed is the city into its tiny geographical area, so compressed by the limits of space that it could burst at any moment) has been released by encroaching development into the water itself — areas filled in and then built on — but this has come to an end now, mainly due to Walter's influence. It was in danger of spoiling his view.

This evening, the Board of CantoCorp directors and their illustrious guests are gathering to celebrate Walter Yeung's birthday. Walter occasionally reads that he himself also doesn't really exist but is, like his building, a mirage, one created by darkly unspecified global forces — Bilderburg, Illuminati, International NeoLiberalism, a Consortium of Triads, you name it — as a figurehead for CantoCorp, which is really an agency for world domination by any combination of said forces. Walter used to find this amusing, but not these days.

The directors — all men, all around Walter's age, some of whom have worked with him since the beginning — chat excitedly with monarchs, ambassadors, industrialists, politicians, movie stars, pop singers, sporting legends, celebrities and socialites. The scent of money, privilege, and power clogs the air with its perfumed smog.

Beautiful young men and women in silk jackets and slim-fitting trousers the colour of port wine, proffer trays of Dom Pérignon and precious sterlet caviar (served on individual mother-of-pearl spoons so as not to taint its flavour), gifts from the Presidents of France and Iran respectively.

In the centre of the plush, clotted cream and ecru suite, planted some five metres apart, stand two large easels. Each is draped with a large swathe of theatrical velvet, one midnight blue, the other a deep crimson, covering over (you can discern the shape quite clearly) a rectangular frame. The guests and Board members glance obliquely at the easels and whisper to each other, but none dares take a peek. There's the sense of a moment, a happening, that will be discussed and dissected on TV and online, written up and analysed in newspapers, magazines, and journals, a scene in which everyone present has been cast as spectator-participant-witness-to-history. It is *super* exciting to be here.

Walter Yeung founded CantoCorp in 1986 and for the next ten years was a moderately successful, widely-respected businessman; medium-scale manufacturing of domestic appliances, some import/export of textiles and clothing, and a number of property and land buy-outs that he sat on for a while before selling at a huge profit. In 1997, on the evening of the handover of Hong Kong to China, he went for drinks after the rain-sodden ceremony with a business associate.

"Walter, why so glum?!" his friend had exclaimed. "You look as miserable as our toad-faced former Governor." He poured him some more whiskey. "Look, men like you and me have got it made! All these motherfuckers bleating about their human rights don't know shit. *We're*

3

the ones who really know how the world works. The industries that have always been the property of mainlanders can be ours. We're Chinese now. Citizens of the People's Republic! Invest! *Invest!*"

Walter took this advice to heart. He was aware that China's future was set on a course of massive growth in manufacturing, so he did indeed invest, and heavily, in construction. He would be needed to build their factories, he reasoned, as well as the sprawling, high-rise developments drawn up to replace the old neighbourhoods and cities they were committed to tearing down. He saw that much clearly enough, but no one, not even Walter, could have predicted the extent of the Chinese boom. He reasoned that, if he was going to build factories he might as well do it for himself rather than for others, so he diversified into large scale manufacturing of consumer goods. He'd made his first billion by the start of the new millennium and now, well, he lets others count his money for him.

The elevator doors glide open and Walter enters the space. He is accompanied by his personal assistant, Yo Yo, a young Shanghainese who walks two paces in front of him, smoothing his passage through the world. She has been with Walter for almost four years, which is, everyone acknowledges, pretty good going. They are followed by a briefcase-carrying, well-built, handsome man, in dark glasses and a sharply austere black suit. His name is not known.

Yo Yo scans the penthouse with discreet precision. Everything is to her satisfaction. With the flick of a wrist she summons a waitress who, whipping her silver tray round, offers Walter the very same glass of champagne that Sophie, Hereditary Princess of Lichtenstein, just now had her eye on. Walter takes it, leaving Her Serene Highness grasping at empty air, sips the champagne — it is superb — and contemplates a spoonful of caviar before thinking better of it. He nods in satisfaction and, only then, insinuates himself into the gathering like a drop of ink in water.

As if triggered by his movement, the spotlights shift and warm. A string ensemble and accompanying harpist are revealed on the terrace, the volume of chatter dips momentarily around their delicate music, then resumes. All of Walter's fellow Board members ignore him. They know full well he prizes loyalty but despises sycophants; they are not to approach him, nor to engage him in conversation unless he addresses them first. They know not to mention business or politics outside of the Boardroom unless prompted. They must *never* ask about family.

None of them, not even those who have been with him since the early days of CantoCorp, feels they genuinely know him. He is less living legend, more a walking myth, as elusive and enigmatic as any deity.

They know that Walter Yeung, as befits his background and status, has thrown a party for every birthday of his life. They do not know that this one will be his last.

Walter notes the presence of the covered easels but makes no reference to them as he works the room, shaking or kissing the hand of monarch, ambassador, industrialist, politician, movie star, pop singer, sporting legend, celebrity and socialite. Spotting a delicate, chalk-white flower — an orchid, the thinks — tucked behind the ear of one of his guests (a lovely Belgian actress) he whispers to Yo Yo who zips over to her and, with a friendly but firm grip on her elbow, leads her out of the room. They re-emerge seconds later, the flower having vanished, the Belgian actress's smile wide but uncertain.

Walter sees the American Vice-President, whom he has met many times at G8 brunches, around the breakfast table at Davos, at state banquets and secret weekend gatherings at the country retreats of oligarchs and other billionaire industrialists. He allows a brief smile to dawn on his face as he greets him.

"Hello, Veep," he says.

"Good to see you, Wally."

Walter's smile broadens. No one else calls him that. The two men share moments of great loss in their lives and their occasional, intimate conversations regarding the particular effects of personal tragedy have granted them special license in how they address and speak to each other.

But before they can begin any kind of talk at all Walter feels himself suddenly flushed with heat, brings a hand to his face and wobbles on his heels. The well-built man in the sharp suit takes a stride forward and moves to intervene, but Walter halts him with a raised finger and the man steps back, as if nothing has occurred. Indeed nothing *has*, except that Walter thought he spotted his own son, Jeffrey, carrying a tray of empty glasses towards the kitchen. He immediately recognises his absurd error — the young waiter's neat, slicked-back hair and rimless spectacles make him appear as Jeffrey did ten years ago, the last time Walter and he were in the same room.

After a couple of deep breaths, Walter is able to focus on the Chief Executive of the Hong Kong Assembly who is standing next to him, and speaking; "…offers his sincere apologies, Mister Yeung, given the timing of the State Visit to Brazil. Most unfortunately he — "

Walter interrupts with a practised chuckle. "I admire President Xi's sense of priority," he says.

As the Chief Executive titters into his palm, Walter leans in to Yo Yo. He needs this evening's planned distraction forthwith. "Time to begin," he murmurs. Then, raising his voice slightly, he addresses those in the immediate vicinity. "Shall we?"

Yo Yo sweeps the room rapidly, her insistent, "Shhhhhhhhhh," quietening everyone.

The lights on the terrace dim, the music fades and dissolves.

The guests, realising the happening is about to start, shift and gather together in a wide circle around Walter. They regard his showmanship with wary excitement, as you would a snake charmer.

"Your Majesties," he begins, "Highnesses, Excellency's, Holinesses, honoured guests, friends old and new, welcome and thank you for being with me here tonight," — he waits for the gentle bubble of applause to pass — "I'm *very* pleased to tell you my doctor is also attending should I over indulge." He raises his glass towards the sharp-suited, briefcase-carrying, well-built man. The guests turn as one but this doctor remains impassive, unreadable behind his Ray-Bans.

"Now," Walter says, bouncing on his toes, "it is time for our evening's entertainment." He surveys the sets of eyes upon him, the polished faces and bespoke lounge suits the bare, bejewelled, necks and arms. The air is crackling already.

"As you may know, for the last few years I have indulged in a certain passion — some might call it folly — of my own: the accumulation of one of the world's greatest art collections. If I may say so myself." He sidles towards the easel covered with the midnight blue cloth and the guests part to form a glittering corridor.

Unbidden, as if rehearsed, Yo Yo takes hold of the darkly shimmering velvet and pulls it. It falls away in ripples to reveal a bright landscape with hills and houses rising towards a distant mountain under a vivid, cloud-flecked sky, all rendered in lozenges of vibrant blue, pale orange, green and white. The painting's effect is dazzling, subtly complex, like the moment the sun appears after a storm. There are mumbles of appreciation, a buzz of delight, followed by a crescendo of enthusiastic applause.

"My latest acquisition!" Walter shouts. "Cézanne's *Landscape, Mont Saint-Victoire!*" He skips across to the other easel, weaving between the guests, his heart fluttering with champagne and trepidation.

7

Walter nods, sharply. An intense silence falls.

Yo Yo takes hold of the crimson velvet and whisks it away to uncover a second canvas, the sight of which generates a collective gasp. The world's number one ranked women's tennis player, a long-legged Belarussian, exclaims: "But — they're *identical*."

The gawking guests swivel from one canvas to the other and back again, as if they are, indeed, watching a tennis match. She is right.

Walter fizzes with barely contained glee. Oh, he is enjoying himself now! He feels like his old self once more.

"My dear friends! At the same time as acquiring my Van Goghs, my Warhols, my de Koonings and Koonses, my, Basquiats, my Rodins, my — my — *Cézanne*," he exclaims, pointing at the two canvases simultaneously, "I have poured more money than I care to remember into a little vanity project of my own," — he lets out a boyish giggle — "the development of a painting machine that can faithfully and faultlessly reproduce the work of the world's greatest artists."

An anxious muttering spreads throughout the suite. He may have lost them for the moment. The splendidly attired Cardinal of Hong Kong crosses his arms. The wife of the Ambassador from Belize covers her mouth with a satin-gloved hand. Someone, somewhere, splutters, "…downright bloody *forgery*." Is this going as Walter planned? No, not quite. A stiff nerve is required, the resolve he is renowned for.

He extends a steady arm towards the ceiling, becomes a lightning rod for their disquiet. "*And!* As a special entertainment for you all, on this my birthday, I have devised a little test. A game, if you will. Earlier this week, I brought together six renowned art experts from the most prestigious museums, academies, and auction houses across the globe. These — let us call them Masters of Attribution — have spent three whole days examining these paintings — these two *glorious* paintings — and have been charged with deducing which is genuine and which the reproduction."

Smiles break out. His Eminence the Cardinal stands at ease. The Ambassador's wife guffaws loosely. The Belarussian tennis player's exquisite shoulder muscles release their tension. So it's a game, that's what's happening. Yes, they will remember this night.

Walter nods at the elevator then, directing all eyes towards it. The doors immediately glide open as if by remote control, and its occupants, the half-dozen art experts, spill out, red-faced and sweaty, as if they have been squashed together in the brushed copper cubicle all this time.

There is an amused hum at the sight of this bunch of civilians whose dishevelment contrasts starkly with the slick corporate veneer of their surroundings and the people within it.

One of them, the director of a world-famous auction house, manages to collect himself, straightening his cuffs and flattening a strawberry blond tuft sticking up at his crown. He tries a smile but his lips are so dry from fear, they stick to his gums and he has to prod them back into place. "Mister Ye — ung," he says, bowing halfway through the name and thereby addressing the floor.

Walter bites his tongue and refrains from laughing out loud, but those close enough to observe his amusement do it for him. They are all on his side now.

"Dis — honoured — no! — *stinguished* guests," the man continues. "I have been selected, um, chosen, by my esteemed colleagues and fellow experts to speak on their behalf as, if you like, foreman of the jury." He has broken out into a persistent sweat, despite the room's carefully controlled environment, and mops his face with a large, paisley-print handkerchief.

"We have spent many hours examining and deliberating over these two extraordinary canvases and I'm delighted to say we have come to a unanimous conclusion!"

There's a collective '*Ooooh*' and Walter raises an eyebrow.

The auction house director, visibly emboldened by this, steels himself and strides across to one of the easels. He regards the painting resting upon it cautiously for a mere second, then turns to face his enrapt audience. "Our unanimous verdict," he says, his voice rising in pitch and volume, "is that this" — he caresses the picture's gilded frame — "is *not* the work of Paul Cézanne!" In a flash he swings his arm back and punches a hole through the very centre of the canvas.

One of his colleagues emits a gargled shriek. A waitress drops a tray of champagne flutes that shatter on the carpet. The guests are riveted, wide-eyed and silent.

The auction house director pulls his fist out from the painting and holds it aloft in triumph, his knuckles glinting white under the many spotlights. He is trembling, sweat now dripping off him and onto the pool of midnight-blue velvet that lies beneath the easel like an oil slick.

All of the guests, the expert jury, the waiting staff, the musicians who've come in from the terrace to witness the scene, struggle collectively for breath, as if the air has been sucked from them and out through the gaping black hole that now exists at the heart of the once gorgeous landscape.

The corner of Walter's mouth twitches. He breaks into slow, solo applause.

"Bravo," he says, with not a single hint of congratulation. "Bravo indeed. You have judged correctly."

At this, there is a huge cheer and rapturous applause. The art experts huddle together in a teary group and hug like a cup-winning team, before breaking apart to reach for the nearest glass of something, anything, to wet their panicked throats.

The guests throng around them, offering their own congratulations, salutes, genuflections, and ululations.

Walter makes his way, unseen, to the elevator and steps inside, closely followed by Yo Yo and the doctor.

The real *Landscape, Mont Saint-Victoire* by Paul Cézanne, bought just a few months earlier for fifty-seven million U.S. dollars, rests quietly on its stand, completely ignored.

As the elevator doors close Walter watches the jury's foreman, director of one of the world's most prestigious auction houses, his raised hand still clutching a champagne flute in triumph, crumple into a pale, dead faint.

Nick, Liverpool — 2008

The woman being killed is lying face up on the ground, her arms stretched out on either side. A man's got hold of one wrist, pinning her down. His face is hidden, just a glimpse of one ear under his cap, and his cloud-white shirt flies up as if he's just now rushed forward. Booted feet set firm, the whole force of his body is gathered behind the knife he grasps in his other, raised, hand.

The killer's got an accomplice, a heavy woman in a grimy yellow blouse and dark skirt, black hair streaked with grey, who bends to press on the victim's shoulder with her full weight. The woman being killed is wearing a dark blue dress that won't protect her from the blade about to be plunged in just above her groin. Her head is twisted towards us, blonde hair trailing in the mud, her open, down-turned mouth a small, black tunnel. She's screaming, but no one hears her.

Nick pulls back to take in the whole painting at once; the pigment thick and jagged, the figures livid against the sombre backdrop: a cliff top, or a riverbank, it's hard to tell; the sky, the horizon, the land, all merging into a void of oily bluey-black. He looks at the label again:

The Murder, c.1868; Paul Cézanne.

13

Maria told him to come and see it, so he'd understand more about the film she was working on. "It's the painting that sparked the director off," she'd said. Looking at it now, Nick wonders what that says about the bloke.

Maria was dead excited telling Nick about the first day's shoot; the horse-drawn carriages clattering across the cobbles in front of Saint George's Hall, loads of costumed extras strolling up and down the Paris street set that took two weeks to build, all for just a few days filming. She'd gone on and on about how great that Marius Woolf was, him who was playing the lead. It was all 'Marius this' and 'Marius that' and Nick'd had to stop himself being cold and sharp with her.

"He strides along with a big hat on that hides his face and he's got this clay pipe between his teeth," she'd told him. "And he's got a big dark coat that flaps as he marches along, not moving aside for no one." It all sounded a bit clichéd to Nick, though he never said that to Maria.

He hears, "Miss! *Miss! Miss!!*" and peers through to the atrium where a group of kids are holding up their hands for pencils and paper given out by their teacher. "Find your favourite painting and copy it best as you can," she calls above the echoing din.

Nick had shared this energy once, the thrill of Paddy O'Riordan's art room, sometimes sitting in front of a wall of pictures taped up for discussion and how Paddy let you call him Paddy and swear in his classes, as long as it was the art that made you swear. It was Paddy who brought art into Nick's life when he'd needed it most: "It'll shake you up and shore you up, Nicholas," he'd said, in his light, singsong poet-y voice.

He used to imagine Paddy as the dad he would have liked for himself, if that bastard Jimmy hadn't already been his dad. He never wanted Jimmy's approval for nothing but he was always dying to show Paddy his drawings. His frustration too when he couldn't draw as well as he wanted, even though Paddy told him over and over, "Be patient lad! Find your own way. Don't be such a — " what was it he called him? — "a *literalist*."

It was in Paddy's class where he and Maria first laid eyes on each other. They were both fourteen and Paddy's group was the top set, filled with those who were being streamed towards further study if they'd wanted. A lot of them struggled, hit a ceiling when it came to their own creativity, didn't have the stamina to break through it and keep trying, or grew to think it was all stupid anyway, which is what they said about things *they* were too stupid to understand, Nick always thought. Not him though, and not Maria neither. She didn't speak up much in those rowdy, chaotic sessions but she was soaking it all in with her dark eyes, Nick could see.

There was a Cézanne taped up on Paddy's wall, but it was nothing like this one, and he remembers it well because it was one of the few times when Maria *did* say something. There were some apples piled on a table, and a jug of flowers. The print was faded in one corner where the blinds had failed to protect it from the sunlight that poured into the classroom. Nick feels the warmth from that light still, the afternoons spent drawing and painting whatever Paddy set up for them. They were the best times of his life in that classroom, sinking into a deep well of concentration, looking, really looking, at what was in front of him and trying to get it down, the only sounds the pencils whispering against the paper, Paddy going round suggesting changes and giving encouragement, his lilting murmur mingling with the fat flies buzzing and tapping against the big windows.

Someone had said that the apples on the table in Paddy's faded print didn't even look like apples, they were more like oranges and someone else shouted out they were '*sodding rubbish*!' There were loud laughs and whoops because Paddy had only just finished explaining in detail about Cézanne's method, or something, Nick couldn't remember exactly, and was in the middle of reading out the words written in his flamboyant cursive — proof alone for some of them that Paddy the Poofter, as they called him, was exactly that — across overlapping sheets of A4 and taped up on the wall above the print: *I Will Astonish Paris With An Apple*.

Maria's voice had suddenly cut through the din — "They're not rubbish, *dickhead*, they're beautiful!" — then her face flushed as bright as the apples, and the noise abated to muffled sniggers as Paddy regained control. For days afterwards, Maria's protest was called out to her in a high-pitched wail that was nothing like her voice whenever she walked through the school corridors.

It was Nick who, seeing her holding her breath in frustration one afternoon, as she shoved her books into her locker, came up beside her and said, "You were right. They *are* beautiful," and she'd side-eyed him to check he wasn't taking the piss before she allowed herself to exhale, letting the air out. He was a goner from that moment.

That lovely painting was nothing like this awful one. What's happening is horrible, really horrible. The small, square label has Cézanne's dates on it, (1839-1906), and Nick takes a moment to work out he was twenty-eight when he painted this, just a bit younger than Nick is now.

It says:

Although uncharacteristic of Cézanne's later work, the violence expressed in brutal strokes of a palette knife is typical of work he produced at the end of the 1860s.

This must have been hard work, even painful, the knife threatening to rip the canvas with every swipe of paint. It's like a bad dream. Like one of Nick's own bad dreams. Any one of them kids could come in here. Any one of them might see this painting. It should come with a warning — if they use it in the film it should be rated 18 — but here it is, on open view.

The label says:

This forceful composition has close parallels to the murderous themes in novels by Émile Zola, Cézanne's boyhood friend with whom he remained in close contact.

So he'd read the story in a book, had he? In his friend's book? Maybe an exposed adultery the booted man in white has always suspected, or a jealous lover who needs got rid of, or maybe a blackmail that's gone too far? Maybe the film Maria's working with will explain the story behind it all, this nightmare on canvas.

A couple of girls come into the room then, just as he'd feared, carrying paper and pencils. They must be about twelve or thirteen, and one of them, wearing an apple-green quilted Puffa jacket, meets Nick's stare for a second, her blue eyes clear and calm. Well, she might be okay now but the painting will upset her. He takes a step forward and places himself in front of it.

The girl sighs, like she's annoyed. Has she come in here specially to see it, like he did? She might have seen the local news reports about the film starring Marius Woolf, read online about the movie director's return to his home town, Liverpool standing in for Paris, and this painting in the Walker that started it all off. She might have said to her teacher, "Miss? Can you tell me where to find *The Murder*, by Paul Cézanne?" That's what Nick would've done at her age.

He can sense her there, waiting for him to move. She doesn't understand he's doing this for her. She must be thinking how selfish he is, standing right in front of the painting she's come for, standing right up close so no one else can see. He'll tell her he's not selfish, honest. He doesn't want her to be scared, that's all. He can't though. The only thing he can do is focus on the label:

The sensational subject matter is often considered the outpouring of his youthful and impetuous nature.

"Sensational?" Is that what they call it? Why should youth have anything to do with it? "'Impetuous nature' — what the fuck does that mean?" He's spoken out loud, he realises, and winds himself back in.

He looks round to see if the girl heard him, but she's joined her friend in front of another painting — a big blue-green sea with some bathers in red-and-white striped swimsuits. They've sat down cross-legged in front of it and are starting to draw, heads bobbing between paper and canvas. He hopes they never heard him.

He's feeling a bit dizzy. Turns back to *The Murder*. The killer's anxious, he sees. The force of the blow he's about to strike might weaken his grip on the knife and he anticipates stabbing more than once so mustn't let the handle slicken with blood — with *her* blood. The accomplice wants it done quick (as if it's just another daily chore before she can go back to doing the washing) and Nick hears her shouting words of encouragement: *Do it! Do it now!* He doesn't want to look any more, but he can't not look. It's beautiful, like a fresh wound is beautiful.

The woman being killed reaches out with a grey, desperate, hand. Her throat is clogged with fear, but if Nick leans in he can hear her thoughts: *How's this happening? I love this man — I thought he loved me — she's my friend — can this be my death? Oh please. Let it be over. Oh please...*

All at once, he tips forward into the blue-black void, but manages to steady himself — spreads his legs and feet to hold his ground — and sees his reflection in the glass covering the canvas, protecting it. With one arm outstretched he mirrors the man in the painting, the murderer.

A thick panic shortens his breath. It's him that needs protecting. Sparks swirl in front of his eyes. The accomplice's hands are pressing on his shoulders, pushing him into the ground, he feels the weight of her on his body, his legs wobble under him, he is swallowed up by the dark hole of the poor victim's mouth, he too struggles for breath. The moment is eternally stretched, waiting for the tearing in the belly before the hot blood bubbles up into lungs and mouth. He too prays for it to be over. "Oh please — oh please…"

The girls' teacher comes in to check on them — "Are you alright there girls?" she trills — and, somehow, her presence stabilises everything. Nick manages to tear himself away and out of the space, his trainers squeaking loudly on the polished wood floor, making the girls jump and stare in his direction, but he doesn't care if they see him, if they think he's barmy.

He comes to a stop against the low wooden railing that circles the atrium. A clanking of spoons echoes up from the café below. The coffee machine hisses scalding steam.

Nick leans forward and over the railing, but Maria's not there. He already saw the film crew outside, saw the carriages lined up along the heavy stone facade, the tethered, stamping horses, the crowds of people, just as Maria described it.

"She's late," he whispers. He knows she's at work but she should never had arranged to have lunch with him then, should she? She's probably on the phone somewhere, trying to calm her nerves. *I've never been a good liar* — Nick hears her saying. "Yes you fucking well are."

He'll check his mobile. If there's no message he'll be annoyed. No, he won't look. But he's running out of time. He's got an appointment he can't miss — it's one of Hartmann's conditions; that Nick turn up every week.

He thinks about the number of days and minutes he's spent doing things he doesn't want to — talking to a shrink when he doesn't want to, coming to see this painting, which wasn't even his idea and he never would've chose to — but knows he mustn't actually count those days and those minutes.

This moment, this right now, is coloured oily bluey-black by the thought of all that time stolen from him; by his dad, Hartmann, this painting, and by Maria.

He wonders, between birth and death how many days, hours and minutes do we spend doing what we really want? The question stretches way into the future and could take his whole life with it if he's not careful.

He slots his fingers into the railing's polished wood groove, tilts his face up towards the glowing skylight. He slides his hands backwards and forwards along the lovely wood that's dry and warm and smooth as skin.

He focuses on the duration of his breaths instead of their number, concentrates on lengthening, deepening, extending them further, but he must not begin to count them.

How many moments of real tenderness do we get? The rare moments of human contact and warmth, the throwing off of clothes, the stroking of bodies, the lying down, legs wrapped round, the fucking, what do they all add up to?

He could ask the woman being killed. She might know. "No, she won't know," he says.

Jeffrey, Hong Kong — 2013

Jeffrey spins on his office chair, howling with delight. Kicking his legs, he propels himself from desk to wall to cupboard to window like a pinball, then shoots back over to his computer. With one click he watches again the moment the man punches his fist through the canvas. "And if he'd been *wrong*!" Jeffrey cackles.

Another click and he cuts to the live camera feed; Walter inside the elevator, that little witch Yo Yo hovering at his shoulder, the doctor leaning against the full-length mirror, super cool as always. No one speaks. Jeffrey can see by the way the muscles in his father's jaw are twitching that the so-called legendary Walter Yeung, the world's fourth fucking richest asshole, is mute with rage.

Jeffrey watches Walter step briskly from the elevator, cuts to the corridor that leads to his father's quarters as Walter strides along, Yo Yo bustling closely behind, the doctor strolling a few paces back.

Jeffrey likes the doctor, with his dark suits and narrow neckties (he imagines them red), the compact briefcase and vintage Ray-Bans. He exists in the tradition of court physician and counsellor; able to ease pain, to soothe and reassure, to indulge in consoling conversation during the night-time's lonely hours, subservient but supremely powerful. He

21

has no need to run after Walter Yeung. If he so chose he could make Walter Yeung come scuttling after him.

At the end of the passage, Walter stops outside the door and waits. Jeffrey watches his right hand opening and closing as if strangling some small animal.

Yo Yo leans over to enter the code into the security panel.

Jeffrey jabs at his keyboard. The door to his father's basement apartment remains firmly, impenetrably, shut.

Jeffrey sees Yo Yo's lips form an apology as she re-enters the code. Once again he overrides the request and prevents access.

Walter's rage gushes forth, pouring over Yo Yo. Jeffrey can't see what he's yelling, but can guess.

Yo Yo nods repeatedly and punches in the code once more, but once more Jeffrey bars them.

With the sudden agility of fury Walter's hand shoots out to slap Yo Yo sharp across the face. She hops back, her shocked mouth forming a small *Oh*.

Walter waves the doctor forward and he enters the code.

This time, Jeffrey allows the door to open and his father slips beyond the dark rectangle. It's not often he gets to direct the action, but it's fun when he does.

The doctor moves to follow Walter, pausing to place a hand momentarily on Yo Yo's shoulder, before disappearing into the basement suite.

As the door slides shut, Yo Yo's composure shatters and she slumps in the corridor, rests her head against the wall. Her shoulders heave and she wipes her cheeks.

"Poor little witch," says Jeffrey.

He barks into the air — "On!" — and swivels to face the bank of screens on the wall. They flicker and spurt into life, though they're

22

looking rather shabby these days. He'll have new ones installed, the best available, when this is all over.

Each individual screen displays a room in his father's quarters enabling Jeffrey to observe Walter as he slithers from room to room, square to square. He can zoom in, out, split the screens, combine them, anything he wants. His ability to hack into CantoCorp's security and surveillance systems has enabled him to form the ideal relationship with his father. For the last ten years Jeffrey has seen Walter only on camera, heard Walter's voice only in his mind and communicated solely in the imagination. It's perfect, for both of them.

Walter emerges onto one of the screens. "Library," Jeffrey commands, and the whole wall blinks, before each screen displays a single image from one of the various cameras there, rendering the space as a splintered, cubist plane. Jeffrey's eyes flit and track Walter's wandering across the disjointed field of vision. Jeffrey used to find this fragmentation disorientating but he's used to it now, his brain able to construct the ruptured whole.

His father trails his hand along dark wood shelves crammed with books uniformly bound in red and gold, books Jeffrey's never seen him open.

Jeffrey understands that Walter, having created this incredible edifice, this crystal palace, lurks in its basement because it was designated the safest place in the event of a terrorist attack or kidnap attempt. But he has never understood why he would furnish it in the style of an English country house hotel cum gentlemen's club; all wood panelling, hunting prints, swagged curtains and frilly lampshades. He could have employed the world's best decorators, designers, and stylists to create the most sumptuously lavish and tasteful spaces ever conceived, but instead, chose, as he has always done, to interfere in things he knows nothing

23

about, and spoil them, insisting on the worst clichés of dubious taste culled from soulless in-flight magazines and tacky cable shows.

As Walter comes to a stop at a large portfolio resting on a stand, Jeffrey picks up his joystick.

Walter pulls on a pair of white cotton gloves and begins to browse his collection of old master drawings.

Jeffrey pushes the joystick forward and zooms in above Walter's head.

Together, they leaf through the fresh faces of noblemen and noble-women long gone, brought to life by Veronese, Holbein, Ingres, then a Raphael study for a *Madonna and Child*, and a Pontormo self-portrait. Walter flicks desultorily past Jeffrey's particular favourite — a beautiful Michelangelo sketch of a man's heavily muscled back — before slamming the portfolio shut. He tears the gloves from his hands and tosses them out of the frame.

In the corner of another screen a hand reaches out to catch them. Jeffrey zooms in, then, on the doctor's face. Finely boned and angular, its planes form a handsome portrait of an unknown man. "It's a great face," Jeffrey says. He could look at it for hours. Does, sometimes.

Jeffrey reads the doctor's lips: "It's time." He has never heard this voice but imagines it smooth and low.

Walter's face contorts and, in his mind, Jeffrey hears a petulant groan.

The doctor nods firmly, passing the ghostly gloves between his hands.

"Very well," Walter mouths, passing out of view.

"Dressing Room," Jeffrey orders. He remembers the harsh grate of his father's voice and, at moments like these, worries his own is very like it.

Walter is lowering himself into a plaid armchair, having taken off his jacket.

The doctor bends to loosen Walter's tie — perhaps more mushroom, than oyster, Jeffrey thinks — and unbutton his collar. He unfastens

24

Walter's cufflinks and rolls up one of his sleeves, then places a small box on a footstool. Lifting its lid brings it to life and he prods at the dimly lit touch-screen.

Jeffrey has seen the doctor perform these actions many times over the last few months, thinks he could do it himself if need be.

The doctor connects a tube into a catheter protruding from Walter's bony forearm, and Jeffrey imagines that dry, reassuring touch on his own skin.

Walter nods in response to something the doctor says, though Jeffrey couldn't see what it was. Past lines include, 'This won't hurt,' 'It should take about half an hour,' 'Can I bring you anything?' and, possibly on this occasion, 'I'll wait next door,' because he leaves the dressing room and retreats back to the library.

Jeffrey is tempted to leave his father and spend some time reading together (it is the doctor, only, who cracks open the spines of these leather-bound volumes and Jeffrey sometimes zooms in over his shoulder, or downloads the same book in order to experience it with him). But he's curious to see how Walter will react to the evening's events. It might even affect his treatment.

Something rises inside him — not pity, exactly, maybe regret. But for what? And there's a stain of guilt too at his taking pleasure in Walter's defeat. Jeffrey pushes it away, but the effort exhausts him and weighs heavily.

With the press of a button, the screens merge into one image of his father's face. It is a portrait much bigger than life-size, as Walter Yeung is himself.

Jeffrey crawls onto his bed and curls up in preparation for sleep, the only illumination emanating from the dim grey-green light of his father's eyes.

J-P, Liverpool — 2008

The hansom carriage pulls up to a sharp, clattering halt. The cab door swings open and the entire contraption rocks and creaks.

A man emerges, his round, bearded face glowing with excitement. He wears a dove grey frock coat and high white collar, splendidly tied with plum-coloured silk.

The passenger alights, the chestnut horse skittish, stamping as he gingerly negotiates the steps. Once firmly on the ground he raises his glossy top hat and, sweeping the air with it in a generous, optimistic wave, smiles broadly.

"Cézanne!" he exclaims, gazes into the middle distance, freezes.

"*Cut!*" J-P shouted, and sprang out of his chair. "Let's go again." He strode up to the bearded actor and spoke softly into his ear. "Guillaume, listen, you get out of a carriage every day — try not to appear so… so *nervous* about it." He lowered his voice further. "Look, it's just a horse; a very well trained horse. He's not going to kick you, you know?" J-P winked at him, then raised his voice so the others around them could hear. "The rest was great, really great. Keep it up!"

A team materialised instantaneously, measuring the light, brushing the horse's mane, spreading more straw on the ground, polishing the cab door. The actor closed his eyes and lifted his face to the sky while the make-up technician dabbed at his face and combed his beard, as someone from costume wiped away dust from the top hat, then flitted off, before Guillaume trotted back up the steps, then down, then up again, practising, and disappeared into the hansom.

J-P returned to his position behind the camera operator. "Okay — once more — just from the door opening this time."

The Assistant Director worked the clapperboard with her now wearisome flourish, called "Quiet *please!*" and silence came.

J-P waited for a count of two: "Action!"

Again, the cab door swings open and, again, the man emerges, his face glowing even more brightly, and tinged, J-P thinks, with a nervous edginess, which is good, very good, channelling his anxiety like that. He may well have been feeling uneasy at the sight of Cézanne, whose unpredictable and violent mood swings could cause such consternation.

Placing his shiny, black-booted foot on the top step he all but bounds from the carriage, landing firmly on the cobbles while simultaneously raising his hat. His smile is wide but hesitant as he makes the sweeping gesture with his arm again, broad enough to take in the whole world this time, let alone Paris.

He laughs, exclaims "*Paul!*" —- changing the line, but of course it's better that he use his friend's first name — smiles into the middle distance, freezes.

J-P waits, then gestures for him to come forward.

He moves swiftly, arms outstretched, readying for an embrace, his grin easing off into tender affection as he walks towards, and then past, the camera.

"*Cut!* Perfect! Brilliant, in fact." There was a smattering of applause as J-P got up. "That's that one done. Let's move on."

The bustle of concentrated activity started up again. J-P marched directly through the clamour and chatter beyond the cordon, along the metal barriers keeping the crowd at bay, past the security guards mumbling into their walkie-talkies, to reach the trailers lined up beyond where wardrobe were coming and going with briefcases and bags, hats and cloaks and umbrellas and shoes.

The Belgian actress playing Hortense was talking to a group of extras, though she wasn't on the schedule today, as well she knew. There was talk, rumours of an affair between her and Guillaume, who wasn't long married to a Danish royal, or Swedish, maybe Dutch. Well, J-P couldn't remember and didn't care, as long as their work remained unaffected.

He was brought to a halt. One of the extras, a fit-looking, middle-aged guy dressed as a respectable bourgeois out for a stroll, was the image of his dad. J-P thought it was him for a moment and wouldn't that be crazy if his dad had got a job on his son's first feature, so he could see him. J-P instantly realised his mistake when the guy smiled a very tight smile, a totally different expression from his dad's generous, open grin. It wasn't him.

He smelled coffee suddenly, would *love* a coffee, and continued on until he reached his own trailer, ascending the dinky aluminium ramp and slipping into its cool, tranquil cell. He went straight to the fridge, took out a bottle of mineral water and a tin of coffee. The scent of it made him nauseous — had he eaten today? Yes, but breakfast was ages ago. He unscrewed the espresso maker and filled the bottom from the bottle of water then spooned a little mountain of coffee into the thing he didn't know the name of, the thing with holes through which the water came, tamped the coffee down with the back of his spoon, screwed it all together, placed it on top of the portable twin hotplate.

He did all this swiftly and deliberately, as if he was annoyed, but he was not annoyed, he just needed a proper coffee and a bit of space and this making of his own coffee himself, exactly how he liked it, had become a daily observance, a small marker of autonomy within the bloody zoo the shoot had become. He took two cups from the drainer by the sink, placed them on the work surface, then snapped opened the window blinds.

There was Marius, standing on the steps of his own trailer — directly opposite J-P's though some twenty metres away — with a posse of women gathered round him. He was wearing the brown, woollen overcoat they'd chosen as Cézanne's signature costume and, in one hand, he clutched a navy-blue felt hat. His face was framed with short, dark whiskers and moustaches, and his whitened teeth, especially when flashed at his fans, positively radiated in the sunlight.

J-P's confidence dipped at moments like these. Marius looked too much like their idea of an artist and, at the same time, too much like himself; his hair perfectly clean and shiny and well cut, his smile too dazzling (quite like his dad's come to think of it) for him to be anything other than a young Brazilian-American actor and, perhaps what was worse, a real life blockbuster movie star.

He'd voiced his concerns about this to Maria, during last night's dinner, but some of those were, in turn, concerns about his own ability, at the age of thirty-six, to be finally directing his first movie, written by him, with the backing of a consortium of producers and funders, many of whom he'd never met.

It was Maria who'd asked him when he was going to see his dad, now that he was back in Liverpool for the first time in ages. J-P told her there wouldn't be time. The schedule was so tight, the budget too small to allow him time off. The look she gave him! She knew he'd barely been home since he went off to film school, then moved to the States, but not that he'd all but made a stranger of his dad over the years, despite everything they'd gone through together.

Was it him, that extra? Maria wouldn't have engineered his dad being on set, would she? No, that would be mad. Talking about him last night, along with everything else they'd shared, had obviously placed that image of his dad in his mind, but he couldn't deal with all that now. There was so much riding on the film and he mustn't lose focus.

He turned on the heat under the milk pan. Before the day's work could begin they must have this fucking sideshow, insisted upon by Betsy, his Executive Producer, usually instigated by her in fact, so that everyone could see the importance of 'The Project,' as she called it. He loved Betsy, truly, but today she had invited a band of Marius' admirers through the barriers and on to the set and they looked properly drunk with the excitement of it all. Who could blame them?

J-P watched one woman unzip the hoodie of her pink Juicy Couture tracksuit and pull down her vest top, offering up her generous chest. Marius hesitated before — to cheers and squeals from the rest of them — scrawling his name across her cleavage with a sharpie. Despite himself, J-P laughed and shook his head.

The espresso maker sputtered and J-P poured some coffee into his cup, added the warmed milk, took a sip. It was spicy and rich, and his stomach grumbled as he swallowed.

More shrieks drew him closer to the window. One of the women was holding a phone up to Marius' face and he was speaking into it. Most of the others were pointing their phones too, taking pictures or recording him.

Around these, a satellite crew swept from side to side, filming '*The Making of…*' for the DVD.

Beyond the barriers a regional news reporter was doing a piece to camera — maybe live? — with Marius and the fans as backdrop.

Another crowd had surrounded this, most of them holding up *their* phones in turn. It was — all of it — madness.

J-P fished his own mobile phone from his trouser pocket and speed dialled Marius. He spied him look up and squint towards the trailer, pull his Blackberry from the pocket of his greatcoat, watched his lips move a second or so before he heard him.

"Yup?"

"Cut," J-P said.

"Sure thing boss. Be right over." Marius pulled the felt hat on and down over his eyes. He jogged in the direction of J-P's trailer, his devotees swivelling round to continue their recording of him.

The whole trailer shuddered as Marius leaped up the ramp and through the door, skittish as that beautiful chestnut horse, J-P thought.

Marius clamped a clay pipe between his teeth and glowered across at him, his glittering amber eyes and agile mouth quivering with amusement. Now, *there* was Cézanne.

J-P was wrong, always wrong, to doubt Marius' ability to become the young painter, because Marius was possessed, J-P knew, with the same blazing impulses as the man he was playing had been, determined to conquer and sweep aside all obstacles, filled with the burning conviction that he could, that he *would*, astonish everyone with his brilliance.

Marius tossed his hat aside, then rushed at J-P, taking his face in both hands, kissing him hard on the mouth, then threw his arms up. "I'm so fucking *excited*!" He beamed and kissed J-P again, softly this time. "Thank you, baby."

Yes, Marius would make people believe he was Cézanne, and they would *want* to believe he was Cézanne, and J-P would direct him closely because his unbridled talent needed directing, and the film would be a success and easily recoup its relatively modest budget and

Marius would gain the credibility he craved, despite his agent's advice that the movie was just too… too *strange*, and J-P would repay the faith Betsy invested in him, and in years to come this film, his film, *Astonishing Paris*, would be written about as their breakthrough work. All of this would happen and, as if to cement this belief, he pulled Marius towards him and kissed him deeply, slipping his hands in under the thick, dark coat.

Marius pulled away suddenly and looked behind him. "*Shit!*" He leaned across and flipped the blinds shut.

"Sorry," J-P said. "I forgot."

"It's okay. I don't think anyone saw."

"You can see out far more than people can see in," J-P reassured him. "You were very good with them, your fans. I was watching. Could you see me watching?"

"No, but they might still be filming," Marius said, "or taking pictures. You never know. I'll be on the internet signing that girl's chest in minutes. *Seconds*. Oh God, I hope they weren't recording that cell phone conversation."

"Why? What did you say?"

"Oh… nothing. But it might've sounded a bit dorky, y'know? Or sleazy? Flirting over the phone with a girl I've never laid eyes on? Christ knows how old she was. *Jesus*!"

"You're being paranoid," J-P said, pouring him some coffee. "It'll be fine. Everyone saw you were just innocently talking to her."

"Yeah, and next thing you know it's been cut and spliced so it sounds like I'm inviting her up to my hotel suite for the weekend. End of career."

"Marius, why would anyone *do* that? You really believe people spend time thinking up these schemes? You're not — " J-P nearly said you're not that important — "you don't attract that kind of bad feeling."

"Not *yet*," Marius said. "Give it a couple of years. You could sit on that baby for as long as you like and then pick your moment. The evening of a premiere. The Oscars. My wedding day — "

"Your what?"

"Well, you know," — Marius waved dismissively " — just, whatever, to maximise what you could make from something like that."

"It'd be useful though," J-P said, with a smirk. "Stop people getting ideas about us. Put them off the… *scent*," this last word spoken into Marius' neck as he buried his face there.

Marius was silent, though J-P felt him relax against him. He picked up the shooting schedule from the counter, began to thumb through it, though they both knew it practically by heart.

He knew Marius was channelling his nerves into this dark hypothesis of blackmail and forced revelation because of anxieties about his ability — though he wouldn't openly admit it — to play Cézanne. They had talked sporadically over the last eighteen months about Marius' other role — that of film-star-teen-straight-heartthrob — which came relatively easy to him even though it was demanding and constant outside the realms of the darkened trailer, the adjoining hotel suites, his house in Bel Air or J-P's rented apartment in L.A. Marius played it all extremely well, and there'd never been any speculation or gossip that they knew of — not in newspapers, magazines, or even on those bitchy websites.

J-P needed to eat something. He took a quartered melon from a shelf in the fridge and the prosciutto that was neatly wrapped in greaseproof paper. Maria must have put them there this morning. God, she was great. He'd mentioned that it was what he and Marius had eaten on the night they got together, not making it past the entrées before feasting on each other. He'd wait a few minutes before assembling the plate. Neither of them liked it too cold.

34

He flopped into his Barcelona chair, facing Marius who had stretched out on the sofa and closed his eyes. They'd go back on set when they were ready, not before. Like Maria, Marius had also asked about meeting his dad — "Don't you think it's about time?" — while they were here. J-P had similarly stonewalled and Marius was similarly unconvinced, but didn't push it. They'd talked enough about their personal histories in the last two years together to gauge that any pressure on the matter of family would be resisted.

When they'd first been introduced, at Cannes it was, J-P had vaguely recognised Marius, made some stupid remark about how they must have already met because his face seemed familiar, before Marius grinned and J-P reddened as the big screen image of him being chased through some trees by a psycho in a ski-mask flashed into his head. He'd thought the film they'd just sat through so generic, so derivative, had been totally contemptuous of its too-gorgeous-to-be-real leading man who, unusually, was slaughtered two-thirds of the way through (the audience had cheered!) before the female-sidekick-love-interest he'd sacrificed himself to save took charge of eliminating the serial killer stalking the university campus. He'd offered a flustered apology but Marius had just laughed easily and said, "No problem, I can barely remember where I last saw myself either."

Also, Marius had looked quite different in person. He was still beautiful, more so, in fact, than he had appeared on screen because there was more, more humanness to him, somehow. His angular features were *extreme* — that was the word that sprung to J-P's mind — to the extent that one millimetre's difference in the length of his nose, the sharpness of his chin, the planes of his cheekbones, or the width of his mouth, could have been disastrous. As it was, he was... *beyond*. That was the other word.

They'd chatted and laughed about the circus that was the Festival, their predictions for the prizes that year, the frocks and photo-ops and general mayhem of it all, and J-P had felt pretty certain that Marius was flirting with him, though couldn't imagine why on earth he would, when Marius suddenly drooped with jet lag, shook J-P's hand with a fixed gaze, and then dematerialised it seemed, leaving J-P feeling he'd witnessed some holy visitation.

Later that same evening, J-P Google image searched Marius Woolf and, after a moment's thought, added the word 'shirtless'. The very first result was the now iconic David LaChapelle shoot for *Interview*; Marius as a cage-fighting-kick-boxer type, his lean, gym-toned muscles glittering with grimy sweat, a mesmerising dick print visible at the front of his red satin shorts.

In one vividly coloured, hyperreal image, his companion throughout this scenario — a cross-dressing giantess in full-length fur coat and gold high heels who was paying to have him trained and kept like some exotic animal — watched him shower, sitting cross-legged on a changing room bench as Marius soaped his perfectly sculpted arse, the hair covering it slicked into dark, inviting swirls.

The final shot in the sequence was Marius handcuffed to a heart-shaped bed in some Vegas palace hotel, it looked like, resplendent in crystal-studded jockstrap, his feet squeezed into the gold high heels, waiting to be straddled.

J-P saved these images in a desktop folder, then added some others he gathered over the next few days; publicity stills, paparazzi shots (some clearly staged, others perhaps not) and, most particularly, some photos of a different kind taken for *Cosmopolitan's* monthly centrefold.

There was Marius, lounging on a very different bed — tasteful, Victorian-looking, with an ornate metal frame — the corner of a luxurious white cotton sheet tucked between his legs. His furry back-side, edged and highlighted by the tan line across his lower back, shone creamy beige in the glow of early morning, his amber eyes sparkling. Round his neck he wore a thin, silver chain from which, resting between the ledges of his pectorals, hung an animal's tooth. J-P decided it was a wolf's tooth, probably a play on his name, and there *was* something wolfish about Marius — the rangy, sinewy limbs, his lean and hairy musculature, intense gaze and sly grin. Of all the sub-categories of queer objectified desire, wolf was the one that Marius Woolf fitted the most. He was not like J-P who was bear cub through and through. This was something else that threw people off their scent. Boyfriend twins they most definitely weren't.

If J-P hadn't known that Woolf was Marius' real surname, he'd have thought it was made up to take advantage of those looks, but Wikipedia reliably informed J-P that Marius was born twenty-eight years earlier in São Paulo's well-to-do Jewish neighbourhood of Consolação to commer-cial lawyer parents who'd sent him off to study acting in New York as soon as he'd expressed an interest in it.

"They never refused me anything," Marius told him. "I'm their golden boy, born after my four sisters and totally spoiled. But they didn't want me to get sucked into the Brazilian TV industry — all those telenovelas and melodramatic period shit. If I was going to act I had to do it *seri-ously*," — he rolled his eyes — "whatever that means."

They couldn't have known how Marius' career was going to pan out, what kind of material he'd be offered and accept; it was a major source of tension between them. But they'd been right, hadn't they, Marius' parents? Or at least Marius must have taken on board their complaints. It was how they ended up here, together, making *Astonishing Paris*.

One month after they'd first met, and totally out of the blue, Marius had called him up, having got J-P's number from a friend of his agent, he explained: "I meant to get in touch sooner but — well, premieres and shit all over the place, you know."

J-P had strained to hear him, through the noise of the blood rushing round his head.

"Will you have dinner tonight?" Marius asked him, "at my place? I could really use your advice on a script I've been sent. I don't feel like eating out. I've barely been at home the last six months."

Since that Cannes party, J-P had put the notion of Marius having come on to him right out of his head. This wouldn't be anything more than an evening spent talking about some no doubt trashy piece of crap. But four weeks of gazing at, and fantasising about, the digital details of Marius' body meant he'd become unreal and strangely frightening to J-P. He needed to break the spell.

J-P almost said, 'No,' with a tinge of anger that was inexplicable then but which he later realised was self-defensive. He almost said, 'Look, the industry's full of cock-teasing bros who just want something from you and I'm not some shameless desperate queen who'll do anything to bask in your glow, or for the slightest chance of a blow job,' but he didn't. He said, "Yeah, sure, sounds good."

What J-P had told himself was that this was a potential *in*, access to an area of the movie business he'd wanted since forever, if only to find out if it was truly as hideous as he imagined it to be. He was the one who'd be using Marius who was, after all, sending a car to collect him.

As soon as he arrived at the modest but actually stunning Modernist house bought with the millions earned from the half dozen schlocky movies on Marius' resumé so far, those thoughts went straight out the floor to ceiling windows, impaled on the ornamental cactuses in the courtyard beyond. Marius was so utterly charming, so vulnerable, funny, and gorgeous, certainly, but not at all vain, that J-P was instantly bewitched. And he came out within the first five minutes — "You know I'm a faggot, right?" — with a disarmingly unaffected smile, different from the sly, wolfish grin that leered out from J-P's desktop. He felt ashamed of his own cynical intentions.

Five minutes more and Marius confessed, "There is no script, by the way." Well, there *was* a script, but he'd already turned it down that afternoon, much to his agent's chagrin, which Marius pronounced in the French way while raising his glass of wine and sticking out his pinky. He was camping it up, unashamedly, and J-P fancied him all the more for it. "I was just using that," Marius said into his wine, fogging the glass, "as bait."

In the end, J-P didn't need to work hard to push those photographic portraits of Marius from his mind, though he had examined them closely almost every morning as a preface to his working day, enlarging them, scouring the landscape of Marius' torso, tracing the peppering of hair on his chest and stomach, zooming in to count and map the dark constellations of his shoulder freckles.

He liked the *Cosmo* ones the most because, with their use of natural light and minimal set up, they felt like drawings, more intimate and direct than the overblown, lurid murals from *Interview* and when, in the kitchen Marius had pulled off his t-shirt, J-P recognised his body immediately, though there was more hair, dark and slightly curly in places — he must clipper for photos, J-P had thought — and his torso was even narrower and shorter than he remembered. As if to compensate, Marius' slouchy jeans, cinched with a broad brown leather belt, were studiously positioned just below the Adonis girdle outlining his hips, revealing the spread of his pubes and the top of his arse cheeks, pale against the very same tan line J-P had already committed to memory.

The ease with which their bodies slotted into each other that night was a wonder to them both, There had been mornings when, sitting at his desk, J-P would unbutton his jeans and stroke his dick as he visualised burrowing into the deep wells of Marius' armpits, imagined smelling and tasting the sweat there, so that actually doing this, in reality, lifting Marius' arms to sniff deeply at his pits, even more magnificent, the scent even more delicious, in reality, licking them hungrily with an appetite he felt might never be sated, one built over many hours and days, as too when, later on, he inhaled the earthy musk of Marius' arse hole before putting his tongue there, had felt like the most natural activities conceivable, these first times practised mentally so many times that J-P needed no direction.

Replaying this, J-P's hunger grew more urgent. He got up, took the knife and chopping board, began to slice and peel the melon, then cut it into chunks. He pressed his groin against the edge of the work surface to ease the weight of the semi in his pants. He had to focus on their work right now, could not, *would* not, half-undress Marius in the dim light of the trailer and suck him off. He placed pale, juice-sodden pieces of melon onto a plate, piled translucent slices of prosciutto in collapsed heaps on top of the fruit and carried it to the table.

Marius opened his eyes, and when he saw what was in front of him, attacked it immediately, scooping up melon and ham together between his fingers and tipped his head back to gobble them down. Melon juice glistened on his moustache and he hummed with appreciation.

As well as reading that melon and prosciutto was Marius' favourite snack — even before they'd fed it to each other on that first night at his house — J-P had also read lists of what Marius listened to on his iPod, the novels and poetry he downloaded, and an interview in which he was surprisingly articulate about the War on Terror. He knew that Marius

40

drove an electric car because he was concerned about the environment and he was still searching for that 'someone special' and, even when this information, so readily available, was wrong (technically, the car was a hybrid), or false (he was about to marry a daytime soap actress who was having his baby), it didn't matter; it all served to create separate portraits of Marius, variations on the subject of who he was, to offer different perspectives on the game they played.

And there had been some initial excitement in keeping their relationship under wraps, but it meant they spent all their time together like today; in locked trailers with the blinds shut, or adjoining hotel suites where they ordered in separate room service and wheeled their trolleys through connecting doors, in Marius's Bel Air home that was shielded from the road by tall pines, or J-P's apartment where no one in his building expected to see a movie star, so didn't.

Marius was convinced that it wouldn't be good for him to be out, not at this stage in his career anyway, and J-P went along with it, though he didn't agree. Marius, given his following and precisely *because* he was a bankable, commercial, bona fide star, could come through it, and his career wouldn't suffer, or not much given the new direction he wanted to take.

"It could be good for you," J-P had said, the first time they spoke about it. "Mark a definite break with the past."

"Name me one," was Marius' response. "Name me one out actor who gets leading roles, not just quirky friends and sidekicks, or weirdos."

And J-P couldn't, of course, but he didn't like lying to everyone when he told them he was single, too focused on his career to have any kind of relationship. The notion of living a double life didn't adequately express for J-P the level of detachment it necessitated and he was concerned how easily he fell into it. Marius seemed to cope with the lies much better, but that was because he was already an actor.

It also meant that, even when sitting next to each other in front of the TV, bowls of pasta on their laps, J-P still couldn't completely forget the images of Marius on his computer so that, when he watched him deftly twist spaghetti onto his fork, the light from the screen transformed him and his face was bathed in that golden angel *Cosmo* glow, or, when Marius was bent shirtless over the bathroom sink cleaning his teeth, J-P saw the same curve of his spine and tensed back muscles as when LaChapelle had him kick-boxing in a cage.

Thinking about it now, it put him in mind of when, after his mum died, it was just him and his dad, and they too would sit in front of the telly with food on their laps. J-P was allowed to stay up later than any of his friends from school and him and his dad watched repeats of the American cop shows they both enjoyed; *Hill Street Blues*, *Cagney and Lacey*, *The Streets of San Francisco*, *Kojak*, *Starsky and Hutch*, *Magnum P.I.*, *Vegas*. Neither of them wanted to be on their own, and neither of them acknowledged that. They'd both stay awake as long as possible, asking each other questions about plot points, narrative twists, surprise endings and character development until, finally, one or the other would drop off. He thinks it was then that his desire to make films was born, as were his other desires.

Even as a very young boy, J-P was aware of wanting to be in the presence of those on-screen men, see a bare chest occasionally, or a brief scene of romance into which he could project himself. During these moments — sometimes only seconds long — he'd scrutinise their chests, arms, backs, legs, trying to imagine them fully naked by filling in the missing parts. But he was also afraid of his dad seeing J-P looking. They bonded through these TV shows, but it created a barrier between them too. Sometimes, J-P's heart beat so fast at the sight of one of these half-naked men, his breath coming so short and loud, that he thought his dad *must* have noticed and would be angry with him. He'd try to hold himself in but… eventually, he began to look forward to his dad falling asleep so he could look freely.

When he'd told Marius about that mix of desire and fear he'd experienced when watching those TV shows, he said he thought these mixed sensations remained a part of his sexuality. He'd not said, 'It's very similar to what I feel when I look through the pictures of you I've got saved on my laptop.' Those words were never going to come out of his mouth, and there was no reason for Marius to ever know about them.

There was more to be found. Someone posted screengrabs from the scene in *Fraternity of Death* when Marius was being chased naked through the campus, the chase that ended in the shock of his decapitation. There were dim flashes of his cock, glimpsed between the trees, in deep shadow and barely perceptible but nevertheless there, if you looked hard, which would be enough to entice people, J-P was certain, because it enticed him even now, though he knew Marius' lovely cock intimately.

In an attempted corrective to the dominance of these images in his mind, J-P encouraged Marius to cultivate and intensify his bodily reality, urged him not to wear deodorant, to shampoo his hair only occasionally, instructed him to come to bed straight after a run, so that the sex of him, the dirt of him — the dried flake of earwax, the salty mucus, his foot-stink and spicy arsehole musk, the damp putty smell of his cum — compensated for the digital images J-P had stored and which enhanced the Marius he had access to.

J-P looked at Marius Woolf now, sitting there sipping coffee, staring into space. He was augmented reality, an immersive, virtual experience, a 3-D, high-definition, work of fucking art.

Walter, Hong Kong — 2013

When the next wave of nausea hits, Walter takes deep, even breaths. He likes to think he has bested something at least once a day and, given the way his party game went, his body mustn't defeat him this evening. This will not be one of those days when he curls into a ball on the bathroom floor wishing for release. No, he will not succumb. Will not be lifted into bed by the doctor, which has lately made him think of his own father carrying him, and of himself, in turn, cradling his own children. The doctor is the closest he has to a son these days. He will be generously rewarded, when the time comes.

He focuses on the wall in front of him, concentrates on the picture hanging there. If anything enables Walter to direct his will these days, it is this modest canvas in its elaborate, dark-gilt frame. Smudged at first by his dizziness, then obscured behind sparkles of white light, it emerges eventually to float across his vision and solidify into a clear image, just as he solidifies when the heaving in his stomach sinks and dissipates.

It is a strange little thing, this painting. There is a wooden table, partially covered by a patterned cloth formed from strokes and flicks of green and red and white. The left side of the cloth is shadowed by a heavy, purple fold where one corner of the table must be. Walter imagines its shape beneath the heavy fabric. It helps to project himself into the image, to place his body there rather than here, to imagine a better, healthier body gripping the table's edge. He feels the cool, clean wood against his palm as, closing his eyes, he strokes the table.

His hand brushes the fruit stand that rests on top, colder than the wood and clammy under his fingertips. The glazed, creamy porcelain rings softly when he taps it. On top of the fruit stand is a pile of green-brown apples; grainy and rough, past their best, Walter thinks, slightly spongy when he squeezes one.

A reddish jug squats heavily at the picture's core, wild flowers frothing from it in pink, yellow and white. A memory of blossom trickling through his fingers flutters across Walter's hand and through his body, like petals falling, falling, falling.

Of all the works Walter owns this little Cézanne is not, by any means, the most valuable, nor is it considered particularly important, but it's the only one Walter can say he has any genuine connection with. He bought it three years ago having asked his dealer, who'd alerted him to its inclusion in a forthcoming auction, to approach the owner and request its withdrawal from the sale. Thankfully, she'd agreed.

The woman, a New Yorker he never spoke to but who, his dealer told him, was clearly in need of a substantial cash injection, had decided to turn to her advantage the interest in Cézanne's works created by *Astonishing Paris*, the movie released earlier that same year. Walter has real cause to hate that film because of its inflationary effect on Cézanne's prices in the international market, though the irony is that he was secretly one of the movie's major financiers.

He can't remember exactly how much *Still Life With Apples and Jug* cost him, but his involvement with the film meant he'd paid twice over for this painting. "Still," as his dealer pointed out with a shrug, "if you want the painting you want the painting."

Luckily for Walter the woman who was selling was equally keen to avoid the publicity a high-profile auction would generate and a quick, quiet sale suited them both. Walter's business dealings had taught him to recognise masked desperation and he sensed her discretion was tinged with dread. He made that a factor in his negotiation and, in the end, both of them got what they wanted from the deal.

However, *Landscape, Mont Sainte-Victoire*, the subject of today's debacle, cost almost double what Walter would have had to pay before Cézanne's increased celebrity status. Walter had attended that particular auction himself, advised that his appearance would be good publicity for his burgeoning collection, and that too had pushed up the price. Ah well, he'd made the main news bulletins all around the world, which will increase the overall value of his estate. The money doesn't matter. It's what he leaves behind that he will be remembered for.

He's built an iconic, miraculous, building of his own and provided the materials to construct many, many more. The Gehry-designed art gallery he commissioned, no doubt an icon of the future, will house his collection and open, he has stipulated in his Will, on the same day as his funeral. From that moment on, the name Yeung will be spoken alongside Guggenheim, Tate, Thyssen-Bornemiza, Courtauld, Ullens, Frick. It might not have been his first choice of legacy, but the more he'd thought about it, the more it came to be the most fitting way to allow his family name to carry on. It will be another grand diversion of the kind he enjoys.

Watching *Astonishing Paris*, Walter had learned what an unhappy, frustrated man Cézanne was; trying and failing to make a go of things in Paris; his secret, and ultimately unhappy, marriage; how he'd returned to the countryside of his youth after his father died, to paint and paint for years before achieving any real recognition. The film starred some handsome young actor who'd surprised everyone with his convincing portrayal of a nineteenth-century French artist consumed with creative energy and self-loathing. He'd been nominated for some awards Walter remembered, though the film itself hadn't been a success. Not surprising given it was a mess; scenes repeated from different angles and perspectives, its fragmented structure that was difficult to piece together, the stark visual shift from the dark, murderous tones of Paris in the 1860s to the light of the French countryside later on.

The novice director had said he wanted to experiment with form to create a work that captured Cézanne's own use of multiple perspectives, his unique style-world — whatever that meant. But it was not a total waste of his money. He'd had his reasons for ensuring the film got made.

What Walter remembered most was Cézanne breaking all ties with his greatest friend, a writer whose name he can't recall. They'd been known as The Inseparables when they were schoolboys and then young men, but that precious, deeply felt friendship had been simply discarded. It was hard for Walter to imagine anyone being friends with Cézanne. The guy was a pain in the ass, really. All that boo-hoo stuff about him being bullied, his father not understanding him, his paintings not appreciated as he thought they should be. He needed to get over himself. The world didn't owe people like him anything.

And how small a thing it was to fall out over; some novel or other Zola — *that* was it, Émile Zola — had written, about a failed artist who kills himself. In the movie, he mails a copy to Cézanne who, like everyone else, assumes the book's tragic hero is a portrait of him. Angry, betrayed, he replies to Zola with a brief note of thanks, and then never sees him again.

There should have been more understanding between them, but what does he know? Like emperors of old, Walter doesn't have any real friends. People he'd connected to in his life, guys like Veep or Cecil Chao, were not guys he could ever pick up the phone and talk to at moments like this. He couldn't show such weakness. Besides, the effect on his share prices if people knew he was dying would be fucking disastrous. But Zola and Cézanne, they had shared everything — their hopes, dreams, ambitions, opinions, desires, demons... they'd become The Inseparables. How many times in your life do you feel inseparable from *anyone*?

No, he has no friends, not since Annie died. He hopes he and she truly were friends, though that's something he doesn't care to consider too much.

Could he have had a friend in his son? Perhaps.

The questions agitate him and the ache of his reflections is worse than the treatment, worse than his illness. He can't bear it on this, his last birthday. Though often he does bear it. He tries to focus once more on the image in front of him, but his eyes dart over the canvas' unsettled surface, unable to settle.

He forces himself to concentrate on the fruit stand's mountain of apples, outlined in brown against a pale blue wall, the same brown used, with a single stroke, to make their stalks, he notices.

The apple at the peak has a solitary leaf sticking out, its dark green almost black against the blue.

At the front of the table, two halves of a cut apple rest in the rumpled cloth.

He notices, possibly for the first time, that the cut apple sits beyond where the edge of the table would be. Cézanne has made a mistake there.

And the perspective is absolutely wrong, the table shown from above, but the objects resting there seen side on.

It's all impossible.

That jug is about to topple over, spilling flowers and water everywhere.

The painting has too many points of view, makes his head spin. It must not be allowed to vanquish him.

He speaks directly to it, and aloud. "Why did Annie like you so much?" he demands, and the question ricochets off its surface, re-directs itself at him, landing squarely in his gut. He takes another deep breath in antici-pation of rising nausea, but it does not come and he exhales, relieved.

He'd funded the Cézanne movie to compensate for not taking Annie's own work in the artist seriously enough. She would have wanted the film to be made so he needed to ensure its existence. Like the painting, it was a gift he'd bought for her, even though she was not alive to see it.

And what does *he* think of it, this painting? What would he say to Annie about it if she were here? It taunts him for answers: *Come on, Walter!*

He doesn't know. He doesn't know if it's any good or not. Most of the major collections contain works by this man; paintings of fruit and other improbable objects balanced precariously on tables like this one, surfaces that don't make sense; portraits of the annoying wife; countless landscapes with that bloody mountain, some quite like his but many distinctly different.

No, he doesn't know what he thinks of it, but something about it seems so — so *alive*, that's the word. He speaks to it again: "You're more alive than me, that's for sure." That is something, isn't it, to have achieved that?

He glances at the touch-screen's display. Not long to go. He knows the machine's pump contains components made by CantoCorp. The level of wealth he has enjoyed throughout the best part of his life engendered a sense of weightlessness — despite the responsibility brought with it — a weightlessness generated, paradoxically, by some of the heaviest commodities imaginable. Sometimes, he feels so weighted down during treatment he visualises liquid steel being pumped into his body.

Steel and concrete and cement and reinforced glass all enabled him to float high above the global economic crisis, untouched by market chaos, untroubled by bank bailouts, relaxed about the collapse of governments and the ousting of despotic rulers often replaced by worse. It has allowed him to create his own reality, to enjoy a life that even the greatest writers and filmmakers, the most extreme fantasists, would find unreal. Globalization has been his great good-luck charm and, in the world created by, and for, Walter Yeung there was no problem that could not be smoothed over, nothing that he could not do, or have.

Except Annie back.

He shoots a look at the canvas from where those words emanated and lets out a hoarse chuckle. "Okay, you win."

If he has a friend at all, he supposes it is this painting. This is the image he looks at when he contemplates his life, his death. It is what speaks the truth to him regardless of whether or not he wants to hear it. Some days he truly misses it, aches to see it, like a child. "And this is how you repay me," he says. It haunts him in board meetings and at high-level discussions. It calls to him day and night. Rarely has he experienced such longing. Perhaps only once before. He knows that, when he communes — that is the only way to describe it — with this canvas, he is communing with his Annie, whom he misses so very much. He wishes she were here to teach him, to help him understand it.

There had been a ten-year age gap between Walter and An-Xie, or Annie as everyone called her. She was in the final semester of her Masters Degree in Art History when Walter asked her to marry him. She said yes, of course, but wanted to gain her qualification and work for a few years, maybe in a gallery or museum. Annie managed to resist the pressure from both their families to give up her studies and devote

51

her time to her future husband, his career, and the children she would no doubt soon have. Walter had quietly admired her for it, certain she would comply in time.

He first saw her at an art exhibit, having been coerced to attend by his mother. She channelled all her spare energy into her only son, and had become totally exasperated that Walter could reach the age of thirty-four and remain unmarried. She insisted he accompany her to any event where there was the remotest possibility of meeting single, respectable women.

Walter had agreed, not because he wanted to meet his future wife, but because he thought the women involved in the art world might be a bit more exciting, racier even, than those he dated in the arenas of law and business. He had no interest in art beyond what it communicated in terms of status, and no knowledge of it beyond some headline figures, names like Picasso, Van Gogh, Warhol, Monet that conjured only composite, generic images of their life's work.

But Annie... Annie had appeared to him that evening like the first work of art ever to make him really feel something.

He'd seen her the moment he entered the gallery, leaning against a stark white wall, fanning herself. It had been an exceptionally humid day, even by Hong Kong standards, and this beguiling woman was struggling to re-compose herself after leaving the outside world. He can see her now, eyes closed, head back, throat exposed; her apparently demure, cream chiffon blouse, tied in a bow at that graceful neck, was, he realised at a second look, see-through, its translucence accentuated by dotted patches of sweat.

She made no concession to the people around her, cared nothing at all for the impression she might be making, good or ill. She was young, and *the young Mrs Yeung* was the phrase that popped, astonishingly, into his head. And she looked so *modern*. That was the word he used most often over the next few months to describe her to his parents, colleagues, and business associates.

"You look as if you could do with this," he'd said, holding out a glass of iced water. She took it with a laugh and a sigh, placing it first against her temple before sipping some.

She had the darkest, most intelligent eyes of any one he'd met — optimistic and brightly alive. When he looked into those glittering, dark chocolate pips that evening, as he tried to sound interested in the contemporary artworks she enthused about, he'd seen the many possibilities contained within the future they would have together as instinctively as he saw the future of world markets. It wasn't too long before he stopped thinking of her as a commodity and fell deeply in love.

Annie did indeed work in a prestigious downtown gallery for a year or so after completing her Masters. Then they decided to start a family, but, after two years of trying to conceive, nothing. Walter agreed to IVF treatment on the condition they tell absolutely no one. As far as everyone was concerned, the Yeungs were a progressive couple, holding off having children until they really wanted. After many months of secret visits to the clinic a beaming doctor had assured them that two of the eggs implanted in Annie's uterus had taken and that she was pregnant with twins. *Twins!*

Walter smiles at the memory of Annie dancing around the doctor's office, him urging her to sit down and not strain herself, as he would do throughout her pregnancy. Oh —— and when they told their families, that was an even better day!

It had been Annie's suggestion that she stop work at the gallery, even though she was gaining a considerable reputation as someone with an eye. "My eye isn't going to go away," she'd insisted. There were other things she wanted to do, like turning her Masters dissertation on Cézanne, highly praised by her tutors, into a monograph for publication. That was a dream she could focus on, later.

At night, lying in bed, Walter propping Annie up and gently fanning her or cooling her forehead with a damp cloth, they would talk softly about their plans for the children and all the things they wanted in life for them; happiness, freedom, creativity — it was Annie who'd included that — education, wealth, sheer brilliance in all its forms, and as the pregnancy progressed Walter would listen and feel for the children growing inside, *his* children, who were going to make him the proudest man alive.

They scrutinised the ultrasound scans of their babies with their massive heads and see-through bodies with spines like strings of seed pearls (inspired, Walter had rushed out afterwards and bought Annie a necklace of two pearl strands, intertwined). In one image the twins — "Two *boys*!" they were told — had their arms wrapped around each other, and, even though Walter was impatient to have his sons with him, as an only child himself it had seemed a shame that their birth would separate these inseparables.

Walter Junior, so called because he was the first to come into the world, and little Jeffrey were delivered by Caesarean section specifically scheduled on a day that augured great fortune in the Chinese calendar. Walter fell instantly in love with them both and found it a wrench to give either away, preferring to cradle one in the crook of each elbow until his arms went numb. He would phone home from the office five or six times a day for updates, sometimes cutting short meetings to get home early to them and Annie, who was truly blossoming.

All this had come to an end just two years later — that was the sum total of genuine happiness allotted to him in this life.

Annie had been driving home after lunching with a university friend who had a child the same age as the twins. The children would play together while their mothers chatted about old times, their husbands, art, Walter never really knew what. Annie always refused Walter's offer of a driver for her and the children. She told him that she wanted to drive herself; "a small mark of autonomy in my narrowing existence," she'd said. It was a phrase he'd never forgotten.

The drive home was a short one and involved a stretch of busy freeway. According to witnesses, as Annie merged with the traffic the car in front suffered a blowout and swerved in front of an articulated lorry. Its refrigerated container, transporting cut flowers to the market, jack-knifed, gliding across the freeway, and gently swept Annie's car down a steep ridge.

Now, as Walter's stomach begins to churn once more, he can't help but place himself in that car, rolling over and over and over.

The lorry came to a screeching halt, its container doors burst open, and hundreds and thousands of flowers, a mountain of them, cascaded down over the ridge, smothering the car completely. Police, ambulance and fire crews were called and dug through heaps and heaps of chrysanthemums, peonies, primroses and orchids, wild lilies and thorny roses, stocks, hydrangeas, sweet peas. By the time they uncovered the car, an hour later, the air was sickly heavy with the perfume of crushed blossom.

Annie was still alive, though critically injured. Walter Junior had also apparently survived the crash, an autopsy revealed later, only to be asphyxiated by flowers, his perfectly formed little nose and rosebud mouth stopped up with petals. Jeffrey was nowhere to be seen.

Another search was instigated, one in which Walter himself now took part, having rushed to the scene, numb with disbelief, as soon as he'd been informed of the accident. Eventually, a policeman discovered little

Jeffrey slumbering near the top of the ridge. He must have been thrown from the car as it tipped over, a fact that had surely saved his life. The infant boy was unharmed and completely oblivious, curled up on a dense cloud of pale pink primroses. Walter took him from the policeman's arms and held him in hands streaked with blood from the pricking of thorns.

He fixes his eyes on the apple in the painting's foreground, the one cut in half. He concentrates on its yellowing insides, tinged brown round the edges, and scrutinises the glistening dots of black that make the pips. In turn, they regard him like the questioning faces of children. They interrogate him, these half-apples that will still be here when he is not.

He takes some deep breaths. He will lose himself in the cut apple instead, as he lost himself in the faces of his two sons in the days and months following their birth. Today, these apple halves look very like the faces of his babies.

During the week following the accident Walter had kept constant vigil at Annie's bedside. He became fixated by the monitors and ventilating machines, trying to decipher in the code of their bleeps and clicks and whirrs the message that his wife would live. But Annie never woke up. When, on the seventh day, she was declared brain dead, Walter was advised to switch off her life support. He told the doctors he needed time to think and, for the first time since the accident, returned home.

Once there, he went straight to little Jeffrey's bedroom, took the sleepy boy from his bed and snuggled him against his chest. He smelled hot and sugary, like a fresh apple dumpling and was his poor father's only hope left in life.

He'd held Walter Junior in just the same way, when he'd gone to officially identify him and, as he'd placed his son gently back down on the mortuary slab, the sickening smell of dead flowers, from the petals mouldering in his throat and lungs, wafted from his lifeless body.

Walter drove himself to the hospital the next day, trying to recapture something of what Annie had experienced on her last journey, the sense of being in control — of "determining my own movement through the world," he remembered her saying. What good had that done? He became furious with her. What had she meant by 'narrow existence?' The selfish nature of her actions hit him hard. She had destroyed *all* their futures.

Before he could enter Annie's hospital suite he ordered that all the bouquets sent from well-wishers and family be removed and destroyed: "There will be no more flowers from now on," he decreed, "not ever."

Then, in the presence of his lawyer, and supervised by two doctors, Walter had switched off the life support machine himself, and — he has never confessed this to anyone — he did it with anger in his heart.

This anger has been the source of the most tremendous guilt, and driven so much of what is good and bad in his life.

It spurred him on to expand his empire and he used its force to destroy those who got in his way.

It was what led him to collect art — *for her*.

It made him fund that movie — *for her*.

It almost certainly poisoned his relationship with his only remaining child.

In a flash of utter, breath-taking clarity he sees it caused his illness.

The painting seems to sharpen and clear, all its perspectives forming a brilliant, coherent whole. "It all makes sense," he says, and in that instant he knows exactly what he must do.

There will be no more treatment. His... situation can be managed until the time comes.

When all this is over — it will happen before the year is out — he

57

will be buried in his family tomb, alongside the bodies of Annie and Walter Junior, interred now for twenty-three years. Those arrangements have already been made.

The plan he is about to undertake will require the assistance and knowledge of very few people, people whose silence can easily be bought. Besides, hardly anyone knows he owns this painting.

What he has just decided is that beside him, in his coffin — or perhaps lying on his chest with his arms around it — will be Cézanne's *Still Life with Apples and Jug*, from which he cannot bear to be parted. He will present it to Annie in the afterlife, the gift he was never able to give her while she was still alive, as a peace offering, an admission that he was wrong.

He must act without delay. Call his lawyer, immediately.

He stands and, as he does so, the painting falls apart before him; the apples, the jug, the patterned tablecloth, all tip and swirl in front of his eyes.

He is cold then hot then dizzy and puts one arm out to steady himself, but this time knows it will not pass.

He thinks he will be sick after all.

Nick, Liverpool — 2008

He's always liked the Walker's bright, airy café with its large, round tables to share and the hubbub of people taking refreshment. That's what you do in a place like this — refresh.

At the counter, a woman arranges the display of cakes, flapjacks, wrapped sandwiches and biscuits. He won't wait for Maria. "She's late," Nick says, taking a tray.

"What was that, love?" the woman asks.

"Oh, pot of tea for one please."

There's a wire basket filled with fruit. They've got those waxy-shiny red apples that don't taste of anything, and vivid green Granny Smiths with tiny brown freckles that are too sharp for him. There are Cox's Orange Pippins. He repeats the name over and over, but only in his head.

They look the most real to him — nicely squat, tiger-striped green and red over a light brown base — and he takes one in his hand. It is matt and grainily smooth, like the wooden bannister just now, leading down the stairs from the atrium. At the apple's base, a nub has grown over itself, sticking out like his bellybutton. He'll eat the apple and leave the core as evidence so Maria will see he didn't wait, that his being hungry matters, doesn't it, even though he isn't that hungry.

The woman who's serving places a small stainless steel teapot on his tray, as well as a white cup and saucer, a teaspoon and a jug of milk. She pauses, then ducks below the counter and brings out a plate for the apple, along with a fruit knife, which she lays beside it.

He pays and, when she gives him his change, she says, "Thanks, love. Enjoy."

He carries his tray over to the big round table directly under the atrium's dome, the one next to the statue of the Roman soldier holding his sword up to the sky. A mum is already sitting there, spoon-feeding her kid from a jar. The table's more than big enough, and he sits across from them.

He steadies the apple on its plate and picks up the knife. Its black handle is lovely and smooth, better even than the banister, and fits well between his fingers. He examines the small, narrow blade closely, its dark, gunmetal grey reflecting the light in dimly abstract lozenges. Nice knives are hard to find. He'll keep this one, slip it into his pocket before he goes.

Nick cuts into the apple, feeling the give of the skin, the flesh, and then the modest resistance at the core where the pips are. As the apple halves fall away, the knife makes a sharp clang against the plate and it rings up into the atrium.

He studies the delicate hoop, pale green and pretty, in the flesh that encircles the pips. The fresh perfection of this apple's glistening insides, smelling of clean greenness, exists uniquely, right now and for a moment only, before it will begin to brown and ruin.

He slices the half in half again, then cuts away the fibrous centre housing the pips and they drop out onto the plate. Once, when he'd swallowed some just like these, his dad had acted all worried and wide-eyed: "Awww, Nick! A tree'll grow out your stomach now, you know that?" Nick lay in bed every night for two weeks or more, anxiety growing into terror as he waited for a leafy branch to burst out through his bellybutton any minute.

He places the knife back on the plate, careful not to make a noise this time, and bites into one apple wedge. Cool, sweet juice squirts from his mouth and trails down his chin. It's delicious.

Cox's Orange Pippins were Jimmy's favourite and that's why Nick knows their name. Jimmy ate a lot of them, Nick remembers, the apples miniature balls of concentrated colour in his meaty hands. He could eat one in three vigorous bites *chomp, chomp, chomp* — all the bits spraying from his open mouth.

Jimmy did everything this vigorously: his jarring, clear as a bell, whistling of tunes made up in his head; lathering his face with the badger-haired brush that Nick still uses for shaving; drying Nick with a rough towel after bath-time until he was red raw; striding down the street so quick that Nick had to run to keep up with him; fixing up three or four cars a day to earn enough cash in hand to go the pub most nights; crashing back home after Nick had been put to bed and screwing his mum whose noises woke Nick up and made him think she was dying. He'd be quietly amazed to find her next morning moving through the kitchen, making breakfast, apparently unharmed, while his dad was hunched over at the table with a strong instant coffee, trying to come round.

A banging noise disturbs him. The baby opposite's got hold of her plastic feeding spoon and is bashing the highchair with it. The mum's tucking things away into her bag, oblivious.

Nick lifts the metal lid of the teapot to give it a stir and snatches his fingers back. He's scalded himself. Using the teaspoon, he flips the lid shut, blows on his tingling fingertips, the sensation one million millionth (what's the word for that? A billionth? A trillionth?) of what Jimmy must have felt during his immolation — a word Nick learned shortly after his dad's death by fire; one that he's never forgotten.

He can't remember though if it always means throwing the body *into* fire. What's the word for when you invite fire into the body? People who set fire to themselves, what's the word for that? Going to the pub for the evening, drinking and chatting away, then sitting in your car after closing time, getting out of your car and opening the boot, taking the can of petrol that's there and getting back in your car and locking it, pouring the petrol all over you before striking a match and burning yourself so vigorously, so fiercely, until all the oxygen inside the car is used up and then the car explodes, what's the word for that?

"Dad," Nick says, and the woman across the table looks over at him. Dad is the word for that.

He puts some milk in the cup, pours some malty brown tea on top and takes a gulp to wash the taste of apple away. It helps if he imagines his anger washing away too. How late is she now? He drains the cup of tea then pours some more and gulps that down too. It burns his throat. He can't get away from Jimmy now. It's that painting's fault, the awful violence in it. He needs to think of something else.

There's a box of drawing implements and craft materials on one of the café tables. He jumps up and goes over to it, takes two sheets of paper, a couple of pencils and a rubber before returning purposefully to his seat. He pushes his tray back, clearing some space, places one piece of paper on top of the other, lining up their edges carefully, then puts the milk jug to one side of the tray and positions the teapot at the back so it reflects everything in its curves.

When they used to draw their still lifes in art class Paddy would choose objects especially to make contrasts between surface textures.

Nick could manage the intricate shading needed for a gnarled piece of wood, for example, but put something smooth and shiny in front of him and he could never get the shape of the distorted reflections right, or the quality of the light bouncing off it.

"You don't have to reproduce what you see exactly," Paddy said to him one time, after he'd thrown his pencil across the room in frustration. "You're not a machine, lad."

Back then, when he knew no better, Nick thought Paddy was talking a load of old shite when he talked about interpreting the relations between objects, the light that existed in the spaces around them, and he'd said so. "You have to draw it like it is," he'd back-answered, "otherwise it's a *failure*."

Paddy had just sighed at him: "Go and find that pencil, Nicholas. Then get on with your work."

Nick got sick for the first time not long after that and never finished his coursework, or took his last exam, but at least Paddy never ran out of patience with him.

He places the knife on a decisive diagonal, the blade pointing away from him. He wants to stand the half apple so that it faces directly out at him, but it won't stay upright so tries propping it with the teaspoon, but it's awkward and, anyway, he wants the spoon in the picture. The apple's inside has already started to brown. That's what happens when you expose things to the air. He needs to get a move on.

Nick goes back to the box of materials and fishes out a blob of plasticene, warms it in his hands, then squishes it onto the centre of the plate. He presses the apple firmly into it. It feels good, certain, this positioning of an apple on a plate, and might be the best thing he does today.

Panning across the tray's contents, he assesses the shapes and their relations, gauging the spaces between the objects and their points of overlap, hearing Paddy's guiding words. He's never understood why this isn't easier for him. "Make your hand an extension of your eye, Nicholas," Paddy is saying "then forget what your eye can see. Let your hand take over." Paddy is haunting him today as much as Jimmy. Nick does as he's told, and begins to sketch an outline of the whole arrangement.

For his eighth birthday, Nick's mum had bought him a drawing machine; a hinged wooden lattice that you pinned on top of a board with paper on it. In one end you slotted a pencil and, at the other, there was a pointed rod with which to trace over the image you wanted to reproduce. The pencil drew it for you, larger, on the blank piece of paper. He spent hours ripping pictures out of magazines, his mum's catalogues, newspapers, to copy. His bigger versions were always a bit wobbly, skewed, but he easily compensated for that with his expert colouring in.

He'd made the mistake of leaving the drawing machine out on the living room floor one night, tripping Jimmy up when he came in from the pub. He'd flung it against the wall and, when Nick wailed at him about it the next morning, Jimmy flung him against the wall too.

With a softer pencil, he fills in details; the pattern running down the centre of the half apple, the teacup's square handle and the beautiful simplicity of the fruit knife, balanced across the plate, its blade the colour of a shark. He won't bother yet with the things he can't manage — the dull reflective shine on the stainless steel, the scummy surface of the tea, the placid pool of milk in the jug, the complicated bending of light in the teaspoon's little bowl — but he has surprised himself by managing to create the apple shapes truthfully.

He leaves the faint, trailed lines he has used to make the pattern of the apple's core as they are — to add anything would ruin it. It still has its pips, three of them, dark as bitter chocolate. One hangs half out of its little pocket and could drop any minute. He works to get its shape and angle right, the tension it represents, then sits back, blows out a mouthful of air. He has not ruined it.

If he's drawing when Maria gets here, it'll prove he didn't waste his time doing nothing, waiting for her. Him drawing might make her worry. He wants her to worry. No, he's being unfair. This job was a great chance for her. She's been unhappy for a while. And if she's happy again then they might get back together.

He brings his attention to the knife, goes over the outline of the handle, trying to get the gentle feel of the wood and the flush metal strip and little rivets exactly right. But the blade is proving hard to get. He can't recreate its sharpness, something that isn't a quality of the blade itself, but is once more about those things Paddy talked about and which he has always struggled with; how the objects around each other affect each other, how each defines its own, occupied, space.

Nick leans in to see how he looks in the blade, to find out what might be reflected of him in it, and an image flashes into his mind, of him picking up the knife and slashing himself across the forearm. It's a cold blue image that makes him shiver and he grips the pencil tight, which is *not a knife*, he tells himself, *not a knife*.

He draws two quick lines in an attack on the paper, unthinkingly, and there now is the blade, as good as he can make it. He starts shading it in, loves the blade's shark sheen, its smoky grey, abstracted reflection of the atrium.

This is better. It's all good.

65

Jeffrey, Hong Kong — 2013

"Off!" snaps Jeffrey, and the screens all blacken and crackle with static. He doesn't want to watch his father puking again, but, gazing blankly ahead, he sees him anyway in their reflective surface, the scene playing out as it has done many times before: Walter leaning over the bathroom sink, spattering green-brown bile; the doctor hovering patiently behind him with a towel; Walter sinking to the floor, gulping for air; the doctor wiping Walter's mouth and all but carrying him to the bed where he curls up and holds himself, whimpering, waiting for the nausea to subside.

The kick Jeffrey got out of watching the great Walter Yeung's deterioration had worn off pretty quickly and his first idea — filming the private moments of sickness and vulnerability, then anonymously releasing the footage online thereby bringing about a grand public humiliation — had faded after the first few recordings. Jeffrey has wished for Walter's death many times, but only in the abstract. Now, when it's becoming real, when it's truly set to happen, he's — what? — scared, that's what.

"It should be me," Jeffrey whispers. It should be Jeffrey's hand resting on his father's arm, holding water to his lips and wiping his dribbling mouth, as Walter must have done for him at times when he was a child, though Jeffrey can't remember it. But it's not him. The doctor is playing that role.

He feels his own body become as leaden and despondent as Walter's and drags himself from the bed to his computer. Working will help. He double-clicks and the screens spark instantly back into the vivid life and joyful colour of his screensaver; the beaming figures of Marius Woolf and Leslie Cheung, posing on the red carpet, arms around each other. Leslie, dark-haired and slight, leans into Woolf, a hand placed on the heartthrob's stomach. Woolf's a good deal taller than Leslie and everything about him — his smile, his loosely abundant curls, the square shoulders and long limbs, his defined features — dazzles. And, *oh*, those amber eyes. At this point in his career, being photographed with an Asian megastar of Leslie's magnitude, one of the first legends of Cantopop and an acclaimed movie actor, hadn't done Woolf any harm at all.

Leslie was known to his legions of fans as Gor Gor — big brother — and, growing up, Jeffrey had thought of him as just that. In 2002, when this picture was taken, his greatest movie roles were some years behind him, though his popularity had remained undimmed, even after declaring during a huge concert that his boyfriend, Tong Tong, was his 'most beloved', second only to his mother. It had shocked many, delighted some, but affected few. Leslie was so adored that even this daring personal admission couldn't harm him.

In their tuxedos and bow ties it's Leslie and Marius who look like a couple, though they never were, and when this photo was taken, Woolf, then just twenty-one and a rising star, was years away from coming out himself. After he did, this very same image re-surfaced to do the rounds on websites and social media, in magazines, blogs and online forums, as retrospective proof that people knew it all along.

His posting of an *It Gets Better* video on YouTube, some months ago, had come as a shock, just like Leslie's concert announcement had. Jeffrey watched over and over Woolf telling how, when he was at school, he witnessed the kind of bullying that drove him deep into the closet, then, voice cracking, relating the story of how he had even joined in the taunts directed at one particular kid who took his own life a year later.

"I have never before spoken," he says, the prepared statement rustling in his trembling hands, "about the shame I feel at my complicity in that tragic, and unnecessary, death. I have a duty to tell the truth, in tribute to all those who have died, are *still* dying, as a result of such cruelty and prejudice. The truth is that, for as long as hatred was directed at others, I was grateful that it wasn't directed at me. Now, if I could go back, I would stand between that bullied child and those who attacked him, rather than join in with them. I'd do my best to make him feel valued. But we can't go back, only forward. So let's all do that. Together."

Jeffrey used to fantasise about Gor Gor singing at one of Walter's famous birthday parties, but was always afraid to request it. He heard his father's response without even asking the question: *What! That faggot warbler?!*

In Jeffrey's mind, he and Leslie would get on so well they'd become inseparable; go to the movies together, hang out afterwards and go for food, take holidays by the ocean, borrow each other's clothes and get on each other's nerves, just like real brothers. But that chance had disappeared forever. Only a few months after these pictures of Leslie and Marius were taken, Gor Gor was dead.

On April first, 2003, Leslie was staying at the Mandarin Oriental hotel, down on the waterfront. Jeffrey had been a guest there himself exactly a year before, in the days when, as his father's heir apparent, he accompanied him to business meetings, conferences and receptions. But the truth was that Jeffrey had no real interest in CantoCorp's current activities or its future prospects.

Walter's extraordinary wealth and burgeoning power had not brought him taste or vision, quite the contrary. The year before, Jeffrey had started to make digital art, which Walter didn't care about at all, nor did he share his son's interest in new creative technologies, that's how short-sighted he was. The more time Jeffrey spent with his father, in his father's vulgar, sleazy world, the more he could feel the pressure, the temptation, to betray his inner life, and the desires his father could never countenance.

At that time, one of Walter's great business contacts and former drinking buddies, perhaps the closest thing he had to a friend, was a man named Cecil Chao. Just last year, Chao, a multi-billionaire property tycoon and the owner of the land on which the miraculous headquarters of CantoCorp stood, had gained some notoriety when he publicly offered five hundred million Hong Kong dollars to any man who could court and marry his lesbian daughter, Gigi.

Gigi Chao had already married her female partner in a civil ceremony, in Paris, and she'd shown class and restraint when responding to reporters, telling them that she still loved her father who, though misguided, she was sure was acting in her best interests. It was a level of magnanimity Jeffrey knew he couldn't have shown, and he knew it as surely as he knew Cecil and Walter shared the same attitude.

All those years earlier, that long weekend at the Mandarin Oriental, hosted by a Qatari royal shamelessly trying to attract Walter's business investment, was the last he and his father would spend away together.

The Mandarin wasn't the most spectacular or beautiful hotel they ever stayed at but, walking through its main doors, Jeffrey had fallen immediately for the plush, understated elegance manifested before them, as if *for* them, and had wallowed in the smoked glass, dark marble, crystal and gold, milk chocolatey sensuality of the lobby. There had been the quiet unburdening of his overnight bag, which was nothing new of course, taken into the care of a graceful porter who was clean-cut and quietly authoritative — a Swiss, Jeffrey found out later — with glossy black hair slicked back and gently quiffed at the front above glittering blue eyes. He was comic book handsome and scrupulously polite.

During the short elevator ride up to his room Jeffrey stared at the back of the porter's strong, freshly-clipped neck and was filled with an overwhelming urge to lick it. He had a vision of this man lifting him into his arms, transporting him to his suite, laying him out on the bed and unpacking him like luggage. At fourteen, it was Jeffrey's first explicitly sexual fantasy and it terrified him.

He managed to tear his gaze away from the back of that neck, only to catch the eye of his father, who was staring at him, his mouth tightened into a firm, straight line.

That night, at dinner, Jeffrey had a terrible argument with Walter about his choice of food and Jeffrey left the table angrily and abruptly. Walter accused him afterwards of deliberately embarrassing him in front of the Qatari, though Jeffrey knew that was not what he was really angry about.

Twelve months later, Gor Gor's shattered body was found on the sidewalk outside the same hotel. He'd thrown himself from the balcony of the luxury spa in the middle of the night. As soon as they'd heard the news, tearfully relayed during morning break by one of their teachers, Jeffrey and his classmates simply walked out of school and headed straight to the scene, as if compelled to gather at the site of a major disaster. A few of them wept the whole way there but Jeffrey, numbed, disbelieving, had been too shocked to cry and was sure they would arrive at the waterfront to find it was all a terrible mistake. Leslie would wave at them from the window of his hotel suite — "It wasn't me!" he'd call out. "Go back to school! I love you *all!*"

That month of April, 2003, was the height of SARS — the respiratory virus spreading at terrifying speed throughout almost all of Asia — and the sight of everyone wearing surgical masks on the street, or on transport, in shopping malls and restaurants, created a vision of civilisation's end.

At Jeffrey's school they'd taken to customising their masks in an act of uncertain defiance by drawing grotesque noses and gruesome smiles on them, a nervous giggle in the face of death. On his own mask he'd drawn an enigmatic, gentle smile, copied from a painting that featured in his late mother's book about Cézanne's portraits of his wife.

When they finally got to the Mandarin, flowers were already laid in tribute, marking the spot on the sidewalk where Gor Gor had been found. A crowd of teenage girls was wailing inconsolably. As he and his friends gathered round Jeffrey caught sight of his reflection in the hotel window and recoiled at how stupid and childish the coolly ironic cast of his surgical mask appeared. Here was death — *Gor Gor's death* — and who were they to dare try and laugh at it? Without a second's thought for the consequences, he pulled the mask from his face and threw it aside.

As the day went on the crowd swelled and the sidewalk filled with more plastic-wrapped bouquets. Some held white balloons in mourning, some lit heart-shaped candles and clutched at each other in stricken bewilderment, others taped posters and photos and drawings and paintings to the hotel window. Jeffrey recognised many of the stock images, no doubt pulled from bedroom walls. One in particular was a favourite of his own; Gor Gor singing into a microphone, head tilted upwards, eyes closed, bathed in shafts of orange and blue light.

By lunchtime, groups of younger girls had begun arriving, all in their pleated, navy-blue school pinafores and little white gloves. They clung to each other and cried into their masks, piled up stuffed toys, threaded heart-wrenching letters they'd scrawled amongst the flowers. The news crews couldn't get enough, flitting round them, seeking out the most hysterical to thrust camera lenses in their faces, inducing them to howl and gabble on live TV. Jeffrey felt he was watching a movie in which the schoolgirls, with their screwed up eyes and silly masks formed a crowd of extras performing clumsy studies of anguish, while, on the perimeter, straining to get a better view, were spectators — office workers, shop assistants, waiters and motorbike couriers — who had come, not to pay their respects, but out of curiosity; tourists of mourning.

As dusk came, the sidewalk played host to a vigil; the lighting of more candles, the singing of Leslie's hits, wailing and crying. Instead of connecting with those who loved Gor Gor as much as he did, who were as grief-stricken as he was, Jeffrey felt increasingly separate. There were a few other boys like him there, but Jeffrey didn't speak to them. He felt exposed by their presence, in danger of infection, not from SARS, but from the germs of emotions, with the filthy mess of what they, and he, were.

The back of that hotel porter's neck had flashed across his vision. Jeffrey could taste the salt there, smell the faint lemony cologne the man had been wearing and which he now wore. He wondered if the porter had carried Gor Gor's bags too and flushed cold with envy. He couldn't stand these stupid feelings, couldn't bear the thought of revealing them.

He'd asked one of his classmates if she had a spare mask, and with a tearful nod she took one from her satchel. He pulled it from its plastic wrapping and looped the elastic over his ears. It was perfectly blank, the ideal protective shield for everything.

73

Now, as the ten-year anniversary of Gor Gor's death approaches, Jeffrey has woken every night for the past week. Every night he has gone to his window, from which he can see the Mandarin Oriental, and considered the time taken to drop from hotel balcony to sidewalk — surely just a few seconds, but long enough to change your mind, long enough to try to swim back up through the thin night air before it merges with the infinite darkness.

Every night he has visualised Gor Gor reaching up towards Jeffrey as he falls, and has stretched out his own hand towards him. Maybe Leslie, who always did things with such a sense of beauty, had believed that to fly to his death would be an elegant swallow dive through the cool city air. But there can have been no way to disguise the effect of the impact; there was surely nothing beautiful about that.

Every night he has chosen to hear *Together We Journeyed Through Life*, the song that most captures his mood. He selects it from his playlist. He has been thinking about his latest piece — his own floral '*Tribute to Gor Gor*', who sings now over the swirling violins: *"In my days of emptiness, questioning the meaning of life, you were there…"*

It will be Jeffrey's most ambitious artwork to date, breath-taking in its digital realism and refinement. He will make people believe they can smell the flowers, though vaguely, faintly, as he vaguely remembers the smell of flowers himself. *"With courage we faced the challenge of life…"*

They'll reach out to take them from inside the screen, as he reaches out now to touch the image of Leslie's smiling face. *"If there is chance for me to live again, I hope to meet you in the journey of life…"*

Jeffrey will connect with all those who still miss Gor Gor as he misses him, and remind everyone that he still lives on in their hearts, through his music and his films.

"*Thank you for sticking by me in the stormiest days, and keeping me company in this journey of life.*"

At least these flowers will never spoil.

Jeffrey sings with him, "*Our separation is transitory. I can only hope that through the fire of my love I live on in your heart,*" until the music fades.

Joel, New York — 2006

It was only just after seven and Joel was one of the first to arrive. From the sidewalk, he stared through the gallery's huge industrial glass frontage and into the space. At the very least he felt out of his depth at these things and, at worst, totally antagonistic towards them; the way the crowd eyed each other warily, the thinly-veiled, competitive edge to the conversation, the practical impossibility of any meaningful interaction with the art they were meant to be looking at. There'd be some hard negotiating to do with himself if he was going to get through the evening, but he'd promised Christa. She was his very good friend and had worked flat out to put this thing together.

Plunging in, the pleasing stink of fresh paint was the first thing he sensed, plus it was freezing, the air-conditioning set far too high for so few people. Still, they'd all be glad of it later on. He pulled his coat around him as a shiver passed through his body.

There was a trestle table filled with tubs of iced water that were loaded with beer cans and bottle of white wine. He waded across the room and swiped a beer, wiping the dripping can on the thigh of his jeans. He cracked the can open and took a heavy gulp. The cold fizz caught his back teeth and throat, making him cough up beer and he wiped it from his chin. No one seemed to notice.

Should he do a circuit of the work now? Or wait for someone he knew to arrive and he could then gauge how he should be responding to the art? He jiggled on the spot before heading straight back outside for a smoke.

He shook a cigarette loose from its red Marlboro carton, pulled it out between his teeth and lit up. Joel only ever smoked in the evenings and the first deep drag always knocked him sideways; heart quickening, fingers trembling, a wobble in his legs, sensations he liked because they took him to the edge of those sensations and knocked the edge off certain others. Beer and smokes were armour and shield in this kind of situation.

He should just finish this beer and he'd be ready to dive back in. He lit a second cigarette from the one he'd almost finished and sucked hard. *Jesus*, that was good. A stream of people had started to arrive now and the place was gradually filling up.

Christa was inside, talking intensely to some girl who had her back to him. She spotted Joel through the window and waved, still talking all the while, about him now, he guessed, because of the way her gaze shifted between Joel and her companion. Great. Joel and Christa had fucked once, maybe twice, when they were sophomores. She'd decided they should just be friends, wise girl. Now, she was trying to get in on the art scene, cultivate some makers, generate a curatorial profile and a name for herself. Well, good for her.

He crushed the glowing stub of his cigarette underfoot and patted his back pocket. If beer and smokes were defences, his notebook and pen were his weapons and tonight he'd come fully armed. His strategy was to ask for subject matter for poems. It was a good conversational opener, though he had some notion of how limiting it was, given the few places he hung out and the fact he barely spoke to anyone over thirty, or who did anything useful for that matter. And it could really throw people. They'd go from being these super confident assholes to acting like they'd been given a hard word at spelling bee and he relished that small, conquering moment. He took a last glug of beer. Time for another.

The heavy tubular door handle already felt familiar to him this second time of entering. As he pushed, the satisfying action, moving through his shoulders and torso, the heft of the glass as it swung away from him, meant the surface tension had been broken, at least for now. He cruised through the low drone of semi-serious chatter and the taste of cool, conditioned, fresh-paint-tainted air (he liked that phrase, he should make a note).

He waved at Christa but, rather than approach her directly, zeroed in on the beers and grabbed a couple more. As he approached, Christa nodded and smiled so the girl she was talking to turned to face him. Just as with his first cigarette of the evening, Joel was knocked sideways.

Christa took his hand, pulled his attention away, and leaned in for a kiss. "Joel?"

"Hey, doll," he said, and smooched her loudly on the neck. She was wearing a strange jumpsuit thing, emerald green, with a wide yellow belt and matching yellow high heels. She'd put her abundant, strawberry-blonde curls up, which Joel had never seen her do before, and it didn't suit her. "You look great," he said.

"Thanks, hon. I'm *exhausted*."

He handed her the beer. "I got you this."

Christa held it at arm's length, between forefinger and thumb, like it was radioactive. "I'd better not. Not until after I've made my little speech." She made a silent scream face and they both laughed. "Here, you take it," she said, tapping her friend's arm. Joel watched her take the can from Christa and press it against her temple with a tight smile. She had not yet spoken.

79

"Soph," Christa said, "this is the Joel I was just telling you about. Our inky-assed scribbler of verse. Joel, this is Sophie. You'd better watch out for this one."

Joel wasn't sure which one of them that last bit was addressed to and didn't dare ask, but the ass jibe was to do with the fact that, on the back pocket of every pair of jeans he owned, there was a blue-black patch where his pen had leaked.

"Oh God, oh God, *oh God!*" Christa muttered. Then, shielding her mouth and pointing mock discreetly to the other end of the room: "I have to go talk to this really rich hedge fund guy I invited in a moment of utter recklessness. Sorry."

"Hey, that's okay," Joel said. "Good luck."

"Thanks, sweetie." Christa trotted off, her piled-up curls wobbling like a tinfoil crown.

Joel waited a beat, then another one. "Nice to meet you," he said, clunking the bottom of her beer can with his. "Cheers."

"Oh, cheers," she said, and clunked him back, the movement causing her to sway a little. That was when he realised she was really kind of drunk. A slow blink confirmed it and she was focused slightly to one side of him. An easy smile came from her, one that seemed meant for nothing and no one. Joel wished he could be wherever she was.

She swapped the beer into her other hand and extended the free one towards him. This hand was small and grubby, the nails bitten right down to stubs, not the elegant, manicured one he'd expected, and he gave it a small squeeze. She was wearing a large ring made from a glass eye set in silver, a very realistic blue eye, the same colour as her own. Her fingers were wet from the beer can so he wiped his own hand on the back of his jeans.

Feeling his notebook there, he pulled it out and waved it at her. "Say, do you have an idea for a poem?"

"A *what*?"

The gallery was rammed by now and noisy. He raised his voice. "A po-em."

"A *poem*?"

She looked dubiously at him. What had Christa told her, exactly? He was going to need his whole arsenal. "Yeah, I'm a — I write poetry. I ask people for ideas, a sort of test for myself, y'know? Adding a random element into the mix. Push me out of my comfort zone." Did he sound like a dick? He had to hold his nerve.

She nodded seriously, giving it a moment's swaying thought. "Poem, poem, poem — I got you, okay, yeah, the tiramisu in Caffe Reggio."

He pretended not to hear her, cupping his hand over his ear so she'd have to lean in closer, which she did, steadying herself with a hand on his shoulder. She smelled of old-fashioned flowers; roses and maybe orange blossom.

"The tiramisu in — "

"In Caffe Reggio, yeah, I got it." He took his pen out and wrote it down. "Is it good? I've never had it."

"You've never? Okay, you, me, tomorrow, Caffe Reggio?" He noticed a teasing, ironical flutter around her mouth that seemed to push through the drunkenness, which might have been wearing off, he wasn't sure, and feared she was on to him and his schtik.

With one stroke she pulled the gooey, ink-covered biro from between his fingers, disarming him, and proceeded to write her number on the back of his hand. She'd shucked off her red leather jacket and was holding it in the crook of one elbow. The unblinking eye on her ring finger fixed him with its cerulean blue stare. She was pressing hard and it hurt, but Joel couldn't say anything because his heart was in his mouth. He had to get all this down.

Handing the pen back she said, "You know, if you used pencil you wouldn't have such a laundry problem. That is, unless you *like* drawing attention to your ass."

Before his voice returned, and before he could do anything to prevent it, she turned and pushed her way into the throng. He'd always thought no one would ever guess that about him, but she had.

He wandered around after that, weaving slowly through the packed gallery, unable to get a grip on what had just happened. No matter how it might play out, it felt like the beginning of something. Christ, the things he could write about *her*, let alone anything she might suggest.

He downed some more beer to moisten his dry, scared mouth. He'd stopped looking for anyone he might know, didn't care either way. The DJ had started up with nothing too heavy; a deep house groove, old-school soulful voice over chunky bass. He was suddenly desperate for another smoke. It might help him decide whether to stay or go.

Once outside, he looked at his hand where she'd written on him, and saw there was only a number. She'd only written her number, not her name. Christa had told him it, hadn't she? Unbelievably, he couldn't remember it. How the fuck could he call if he didn't know her name?

Swamped with a real fear that he could screw this up he threw his half-smoked cigarette down and plunged back in to locate Christa, to ask her the name of the girl she'd introduced him to, maybe the name of his future, when he was arrested — there was no other word for it — by a large painting, a nude, of her.

What was he looking at? A wide, angular face drawn in pale lilac wash that darkened across her shoulders becoming a deep violet at her breasts. Two blank ovals of bright blue for eyes. Her light green knees were raised to cover her stomach, her legs fading at the ankles, all the way to nothing where the feet should have been. Hands were apricot laid over pink, and fingernails, barely there in reality, were here vivid streaks of dripped red. On one of her fingers another blank blue oval made the glass eye ring that glared as provocatively from the canvas as the real one, before.

The overall thinness of the pigment washed out the strange, unreal, colours until they all but dissolved, or emerged like stains. Her freely open, lilac-grey mouth seemed to want to say something about joy, or about life — Joel wasn't certain. He only hoped he'd get the chance to find out.

He spotted a label beside the painting and leaned in to read it:

Self-Portrait: Sophie #1

So, she was a painter, and a good one — as much as he could tell. He couldn't do this. It was too much. He should just rub her number off his hand right there and then and that would be the end of any ideas he might have about them, or the future.

Instead, he reached back into his pocket for his notebook and pen, embarrassed now by his ridiculous, ink-stained ass that he immediately resolved to change. He'd throw away all his fucking jeans and buy some new ones, and some pencils too, like she suggested.

Despite himself, despite his concerns, he copied the number into his book, underlining it twice, couldn't risk its erasure from his body, and, above it, scribbled *Sophie #1*, before tossing the ink-blocked biro away.

As he jammed the notebook back into his stupid pocket, he became aware of some kind of commotion above the hubbub of what was by now a fully-fledged art happening. He felt a space opening up behind and turned to meet it.

The crowd was bubbling, swelling, in his direction, cameras flashing round the edges.

There was Christa, leading some young, good-looking guy, round by the elbow, in triumph. It was him they were all taking pictures of. Had Christa worked some magic, got someone famous to come to the show and parade around? She was going to make it, he could tell.

They came to a stop beside Joel, right in front of *Sophie #1*, and Christa made this sweeping arm gesture, really like a magician whose escape from a submerged, padlocked trunk generates a collective gasp. "And *this*," she said to her trophy companion, "is the star of the show. Don't you think?"

Christa hadn't seen Joel standing there, and Sophie was nowhere around, he noticed. She was missing her big moment.

Joel stared at the guy, who regarded the painting with a gentle grin. He wasn't just good-looking, he was kind of astonishing. His skin shone under the gallery's dimmed lights and dark, loose curls formed this definite — what? — *aura*, or something, around his angular, equine features, his face as dreamily gorgeous as Sophie's was.

Joel immediately visualised her and this guy together; a perfect couple of demi-gods. He'd be hard pressed to choose between them.

He felt crushed, wanted to smash his own, horrible face in, and to do it in front of her self-portrait hanging right here in front of him.

It was definitely time to leave, go home and sleep it all off, wake up to a different day full of potential and possible fresh starts. Or he could stay, see how it all panned out? He didn't know what to do.

J-P, Liverpool — 2008

"Talk me through it," J-P said, rinsing the coffee cups. "What's on your mind at this point?"

"So," Marius sighed, "I'm wandering the streets of Paris, all antsy because the Academy won't let me in and the Salon won't show my work and — "

"Not *wandering*," J-P said, turning to face him. "Stalking. You're the lone wolf, remember? You could be a mad man or a genius, or both, and they can't handle it. You frighten and confuse people, so they laugh at you."

"I remember. And I'm pissed at Émile."

"At him, at the world. You're angry, underneath, at what he's become since he moved to Paris. You *know* all this, Marius."

"Yeah, I know it. I know it. I'm just nervous is all." Marius got up and went to the window, opened the blinds. "I wish we were in your real life actual Paris, France," he murmured.

"That's all well and good," J-P said, drying his hands, "but even with the increased budget your golden presence on set has granted us, we still couldn't afford that. Anyway, no one will be able to tell the difference. You tell people it's Paris and Paris is what they see. It's called the magic of cinema, dummy. Besides," J-P said, slinking behind Marius to put his arms around his waist, "you just want a trip to Paris. I'm sure that's why you agreed to do the movie. If only they'd told you we were using Liverpool when you signed the contract."

"You got that right," said Marius, softly. "What other reason would there be for doing this pile of pretentious shit?" He turned and snatched at J-P's hands. "Apart from working with cinema's bright new hope."

"Oh, is that what I am…?"

"M-hm…"

They kissed and Marius pushed J-P's hand down inside his trousers and widened his stance to allow J-P to feel around inside. He began to unbutton himself.

J-P spoke into their kiss: "Hey, hey, hey. There is the small matter of the day's schedule to get through. And did you forget you opened the blinds."

Marius pulled back with an uneasy grin and sat back down on the couch. "I'm going to do my meditation, get myself ready."

"Sure. Of course.

When Marius closed his eyes, J-P continued clearing away the plates, the food, the coffee maker. "You're going to be great, Marius," he called over his shoulder.

"Yeah, yeah, I know," Marius murmured.

"Did I tell you how perfect you are yet today?"

"Shhhhh…"

It was six months into their relationship when Marius had been invited to New York to take part in an improvised piece of theatre. Every night, a different performer starred in the two-hander, alongside the guy who'd devised it. Word of its inventive brilliance spread and stage legends and movie icons were queueing up to be in it. Though

Marius was neither of these, he got his agent to lobby for the chance, his participation potentially bringing in a different kind of audience.

J-P had lied to Betsy when he invited her to the show with him, claiming this was the only night he could get tickets. "Are you kidding me?" she'd exclaimed when he called her. "I'm amazed you could get seats at all." When they took their places along with the rest of the excited audience, they'd seen Marius waiting on the front row, eyes closed, meditating, looking just as he did right now, on the sofa in J-P's trailer.

What if Marius was terrible? He had talent but it was curbed by the work he'd been offered so far. They'd expounded at length to each other about their aspirations to work with serious, thoughtful scripts, their shared ambitions to create ground-breaking, innovative work, combined with a desire to be hugely rich and successful, but J-P was seeing Marius put all that to the test while having to pretend they weren't lovers.

The lights had gone down and Marius was introduced, first as himself and then in his role as an ordinary audience member being called to participate in a stage hypnotist's act. The guy playing the hypnotist fed lines of dialogue to Marius through an earpiece, or spoke to him directly, telling Marius exactly what to say and do. All the machinery of the theatrical process was exposed and there was no room for suspension of disbelief, and yet it happened. Despite the workings being totally visible, J-P was convinced he was seeing what he was told he was seeing. They all felt it.

The story involved the suicide of a young man, the son of Marius' character, and had real emotional punch. The hypnotist was the son's secret lover, his partner, a fact revealed to the audience early on. These two men — connected by their love for the same person who'd felt unable to carry on living — were meeting for the first time, on stage.

At one point, Marius was fed a monologue line by line, and, as soon as the words were given to him, before he'd had time to process them, he'd started to cry. "I wasn't *acting*," he told J-P later, in bed. "It was like I was experiencing the actual situation, the real emotions, as myself, while being someone else — not playing it, but transformed into this ordinary guy, grieving for the son who'd killed himself."

It was then Marius told him the story of the boy in his school, who killed himself. He was bullied for being bookish, unavoidably femme, and not only in school either. "He'd come to class sometimes with marks and bruises on him, and we all knew why. His dad was a bastard. I tried to get my own parents to take him in, but they refused."

This boy, Marius said, had swallowed a bottle of his mom's sleeping pills, then must have changed his mind because he called an ambulance himself. "He told the operator, *'I've done something stupid'*," Marius said, tearfully. The paramedics had got there quick enough but he died on the way to the hospital. "If I thought he really wanted to die, J-P, I'd be okay with it, respect his choice. But he didn't want to die at all. He must have been so scared." He'd cried uncontrollably then, a full-on release, and J-P held onto him until he fell asleep.

For J-P, the other transformation that night, a revelation really, was that Marius became the fully living person J-P knew now and was in a serious relationship with, the guy he loved and who, he was pretty sure, loved him. Of course he was not the Marius in those magazines, chatting shit on *E!* at film premieres, glinting in the popping flashes, not flinching once as paparazzi and fans bayed, *"Marius! Marius! Marius!"*

Stupidly, it had taken J-P that long for him to know Marius as the desperately searching, intelligent, funny, lonely, lovely man he was, and he'd seen all this when Marius was pretending to be someone else.

Betsy called him early the next morning, while Marius was still sleeping. "Listen, don't freak out at what I'm about to say. I think we should screen test Marius Woolf for the part of Cézanne."

88

He'd heard Betsy out as he padded into the kitchen and began to make his coffee. Both she and Su Lin, the casting director, would expect him to protest, J-P knew, and Betsy's suggestion *was* genuinely shocking. He liked the idea of them working together, seeing him every day, but he could give him a minor role and they'd still have that. He'd never really considered Marius could play Paul.

J-P duly ranted half-heartedly down the phone, banging dishes around the sink for special effect, until Betsy mentioned the possibility of the very tight-bordering-on-the-impossible budget doubling if Marius was brought on board in the leading role. "It's a risk," she told him, "but maybe one we can't afford not to take." J-P had allowed her to puncture his own performance so that he could in turn allow Betsy to mollify him by granting certain concessions about the final edit along the way, until they reached a satisfactory agreement.

Marius had finally surfaced about midday and, before anything else, J-P said, "Check your messages."

It was Marius who decided they shouldn't see each other for the next two weeks, until after the screen test. "I really want this gig, baby. You get that, don't you? For me. For us."

They focused on the mutual benefit to their careers being dangled in front of them — the credibility Marius craved and the breakthrough J-P wanted, while maintaining some level of independence. But who knew what it might mean for their burgeoning relationship?

Marius had done his research, talked intelligently about Cézanne's early life and his work, though he'd only taken a mild interest during the previous weeks when J-P had lectured him about the film's subject. Just the night before the start of their temporary separation, they'd gone out for dinner and created a bit of a scene.

"Okay, I'll admit I've had my doubts," Marius admitted, "but now

I can see the project's potential and what it is you're trying to do with it. The title's a sticking point for me though. Can't you change it?"

"No I fucking well *can't!*" J-P cried. He was nervous too and had drunk two and a half glasses of wine, fast, on an empty stomach.

Cut to the other diners turning round to stare at the young guy in those movies they couldn't remember the names of, who must be brainstorming about a new script idea or something.

"For your information," J-P went on, "*Astonishing Paris* refers to Cézanne's famous pronouncement that he will astonish Paris with an apple. He's going to make the still life the centre of his artistic endeavours, alter people's perception of the world by painting apples that are more true than an apple — and not because they're a — a photo-realistic reproduction, but the opposite. They'll draw attention to the fact that they aren't apples, while still being the most appley apples imaginable. He's going to shake people so violently they'll see things differently, the way he wants."

Marius had nodded throughout, and simply said, "Yeah, I remember all this. You told me already."

"Well, I want my movie to do the same," J-P said, downing more wine. "No biopic made after this will follow the same rules as before, and any that do will be obsolete. I'll change film, like Cézanne changed painting."

Cut to Marius raising an eyebrow, and laughing at him.

For his screen test Marius had slicked his hair back and grown a straggly beard. He still looked sexy as hell, which was kind of wrong but an important aspect of any movie protagonist, J-P conceded. And he'd tried way too hard at being 'period' — affecting a weird, clipped mid-Atlantic accent to indicate the past, or Europe, or culture, or all of those at once — before, to everyone's great relief, Su Lin interrupted and instructed him to speak in his own voice.

As Marius continued with his speech, taken from a scene in which he and Émile were arguing about why Paul felt he had to leave Paris and return to Aix-en-Provençe, it became clear that what Marius *had* understood, with an instinctual brilliance, was that to astonish others you must, yourself, be astonished *by* yourself.

He'd tapped directly into this young man's desires, a sense of amazement at his own potential, mixed with an actual fear of it, and he *became* it, transformed into a Paul Cézanne who quivered with frustration at the possibility that he, and he alone, understood the world, that he was a prophet to whom no one listened, who would be mocked and miserable forever, scared for himself while at the same time knowing this is the only way he can exist, astonished at the fact of being alive during this moment, the overwhelming present, when things are changing beyond measure, and not only is he a part of it — he *is* it.

At the end of the test, after Marius-as-Paul had stormed out of the room, exasperated by his dearest friend's expressions of love for Paris and the people in it, a love that appeared to be stronger than that for his friend, J-P, Betsy and Su Lin all sat in silence, until Su Lin eventually said, "Did we *really* just see that?"

During their subsequent discussion Su Lin expressed her deep reservations, said that surely Marius was simply not the right actor for this movie, and that she struggled to imagine him pulling the whole thing off, or she worried that their 'natural audience' — that was her phrase — would be put off at the very idea of him playing Cézanne, though the room was still crackling with the electricity of what they'd witnessed, she said.

J-P hung back a bit until, finally, he whispered, "But he just *was* Paul, wasn't he?" and that was the clincher. He'd already shown himself as someone willing to listen to others' ideas by agreeing to the test in the first place, that he was open to compromise and not simply some pole-up-his-ass auteur but a passionate filmmaker with real commercial sense and, as Su Lin told him later, over celebratory drinks, "We really respect you for that."

What she and Betsy couldn't know was that J-P had been even more blown away than they were, because he knew that, like Paul Cézanne, Marius struggled with a level of anxiety that could easily prevent him becoming the artist he truly wanted to be.

Like Paul's craving the approval of the Paris Salon, while affecting to reject it, Marius wanted the praise from critics and the blessings of his parents, while doubting his desire and capacity to play the roles that would garner him this, and fearing rejection or ridicule from the world.

Despite these issues, perhaps because of them, the moment any camera was pointed at him — even just a fan's phone — Marius transformed into a beautiful, luminous being, emitting an invisible beam of glorious, substance-altering, universal energy.

Tapping into these rich, unresolved contradictions, J-P knew, could elicit from his star a really great portrayal of an artist as a troubled young man, and selfishly, cravenly, he was determined to harness and exploit all of that despair. It would be, truly, astonishing.

Jeffrey, Hong Kong — 2013

Jeffrey clicks on the folder of found images from Leslie's funeral. He's gathered many over the years, from different online sources. In all of them, Hong Kong is washed out and gloomy, the sky grey and low, as it was on that day. Rows and rows of masked schoolgirls line the streets in their standard uniforms of navy blue tunic, white blouse with a red bow tied at the neck, white socks pulled up just below the knee, black patent leather shoes and little white gloves. In the preceding days many of them had come together, on the streets and in group chats, or in various online forums, to share their personal stories, as well as special, individual, love for Gor Gor, chorusing his songs, exchanging soft toys, keepsakes, memories, all for their idol's sake.

Jeffrey had spoken to no one, had wanted only to watch and listen, to store it all up.

Much to his relief, Walter was away on a business trip during the whole period. It meant not having to account for his movements, his moods, his visible emotions.

Could he have told his father that Leslie's suicide had taken away Jeffrey's only hope of true happiness in life? That in his dying flight,

Gor Gor had become all things to Jeffrey, including the future he would never have? No, he couldn't say this.

What would a man like Walter — such a rough, vulgar, unfeeling man — say about what was going on inside his son? And what could Jeffrey himself say about it? He was beginning to think he might be better off alone.

The day before the funeral, the roads surrounding the Mandarin Oriental had been closed off. Heavy rain, combined with the sultry heat, meant the sidewalk's flowers were starting to spoil. As soon as he'd exited the subway, Jeffrey smelled the cloying, damp stench of them filling the air with a sweet miasma. But when the authorities had tried to clear them away there was nearly a riot, so febrile was the crowd, and the police retreated.

That evening, those waiting were allowed into the Hong Kong Funeral Home to pay their respects. Jeffrey had waited in line for he couldn't remember how many hours, while Gor Gor's music was piped through loudspeakers. This only worked to make the crowd more hysterical and Jeffrey felt, in turn, even more distant from them.

Once inside, the funeral parlour looked so beautiful that Jeffrey and everyone around him gasped as they entered, sucking in the protective anti-SARS masks they all still wore. The walls were decorated in white pleated silk and there were banks of wreaths and garlands, three, four deep, along all sides. The gleaming bronze coffin was covered with flowers and, above it, a widescreen TV showed pop videos, interviews, and a montage of Leslie's best movie-scene clips on a loop. There was Gor Gor, singing, smiling, blowing kisses to all of them. They had come to pay their respects, but it was impossible to believe he was gone.

Jeffrey scrolls through the photographs until he finds the one he wants. In this image, the coffin, crowned with a gigantic spray of white lilies, is being lifted onto the shoulders of six broad pallbearers in white tuxedos, still discernibly handsome behind their green hospital masks.

Caught up in the throng, he'd heard the reaction to the funeral cortege before he saw it; the clapping and sobbing and wailing, people crying, shouting, *"We love you Gor Gor!"*, *"We miss you!"*, *"Gor Gor why did you leave us?"* And he'd been shocked when, instead of the large, black, shiny hearse he was expecting, a transit van, clad in white flowers like a parade float, and with a photo of Leslie facing out through the windshield, crawled around the corner and came to a halt.

As the van's rear doors opened Jeffrey was still convinced that out would jump the radiant, un-smashed Leslie they all knew and loved, waving and smiling at everyone. Instead, the heavy coffin — monumental for someone so small — was rolled out. As it appeared, a tangle of arms obscured Jeffrey's view, all raised, not in salute, but holding cameras and cell phones to record the moment.

Then, a row of black limousines had pulled up and Tong Tong, Gor Gor's 'most beloved', emerged from the first one. In their first public statement after the suicide, Gor Gor's stricken family had even been bold enough to describe Tong Tong as 'Leslie's surviving spouse'.

As Tong Tong made his way across the street, he was shored up by Leslie's sister on one side, and his personal assistant on the other. He looked so elegant, so brave. All three wore dark, sleek suits, their mouths covered by black silk scarves, transformed into a living tableau of grief.

In the years since, Jeffrey has come to realise that the funeral of the Gor Gor he'd never met, his elder brother, had been a substitute for that of his mother and of Walter Junior. His numbing grief, his silent wanderings, his search for connection with Leslie's other devotees, were all because he hadn't been able to attend his own mother's funeral, nor grieve for his unremembered real brother.

His distressing lack of recognisable feeling, his sense of distance from the crowds and what was happening around him, was the same response to growing up without a mother and brother he didn't even remember, but whose absence hung over him and his father as a weighted presence. Soon, he'll be the only one left and, though Leslie's music comforts him, the fact is there'll be no Gor Gor to help him through.

He zooms into the image and pans across the crowd to find what he's looking for. There, just to one side of the procession and craning to get a better look, eyes only just visible above his surgical mask, is the fifteen-year-old Jeffrey Yeung. It is the last photo ever taken of him, and it makes his heart ache.

In the Buddhist tradition, a dead person's soul remains in limbo until the 49th day, when it finally comes to rest, freed from the world and totally at peace. Jeffrey had consoled himself with the idea of Gor Gor's spirit still being out in the world somewhere, as if it meant the chance of him returning. Leslie's soul at peace meant he couldn't come back, though Jeffrey wouldn't want him to remain in a state of unhappiness, the same state that led him to leap from that hotel window. It would be good for him to be at peace.

On Leslie's 49th day, May 18th, 2003, he went early to Leslie's home to leave there a card he'd laboured over all that time, one with flowers expertly reproduced.

A few other girls and boys were already there, huddled together and crying quietly. Some laid plates of Gor Gor's favourite food and sweets out on the sidewalk, while others spoke softly, intimately, to pictures of him.

Jeffrey did the same, whispering into the film still from *Happy Together* he'd brought with him, of Leslie in bed with Tony Leung: "It's time for you to go, dear one." The way he tells the story to himself now, it was at this very moment of saying that line that his decision was made.

96

He'd seen a news report on the phenomenon of Hikikomori and it had made a deep impression upon him. Though described as being predominantly a Japanese concern, in China, South Korea, and other countries too, teenagers and young men were withdrawing into their rooms and refusing to come out.

Many of the Hikikomori expressed how they couldn't stand the unbearable social pressures to conform and that the only act of rebellion open to them was to lock themselves away, escaping into their worlds of computer games and virtual reality, chatrooms and Internet forums, where they felt more free, more able to be themselves. They did so safely in the knowledge that the potential embarrassment to their families protected them because their parents would rather go along with their wishes than become the subjects of idle gossip and terrible scandal.

The notion of shutting himself away had not occurred to Jeffrey at the time of watching the report, though he now thinks that he'd simply repressed this desire, like he repressed all his desires.

After the final coming to rest of Leslie's soul, he knew it was the right thing for him to do; a way of leaving the world behind that was not as extreme as Gor Gor's tragic act.

And so that day became Jeffrey's own 49th day; the last day he went outside.

Marius, Liverpool — 2008

He tries once more to focus, to focus in on his breathing, only. Always a challenge, his mind wandering all over the place, and one he sometimes meets, but not today. Maybe never again.

In his middle-of-the-night, spiralling out of control, crazy episode, he'd decided to call a surprise press conference first thing this morning, before the day's shooting had begun. In this half-imagined, half-dreamed scenario, he would tell the assembled media that he was gay and J-P would be so totally pissed at him he'd end their relationship, which would mean not having to do it himself. But, come the actual morning, of course he'd lost his nerve.

That local news crew are still outside though. He could stroll right on over to the edge of the set, easy as anything, and give that reporter a live, straight-to-camera, world exclusive. No, he won't. He won't fuck up the project, but contain and channel the hurt, his anger, into the scene he's about to play, into the agitated despair that powers Paul Cézanne as he storms past the Salon from which he's barred.

Taking a deep breath in, he lets the air out as a controlled ribbon coloured sky-blue and wrapping itself around him. But it soon dissolves and he knows there's really no point in trying today. He'll let his mind go where it will.

So he replays last night's scene in which he flips open J-P's laptop to remind himself of the painting, of *The Murder*, because that was what's swirling around in Cézanne's mind at this time, and spotting, on the desktop, a folder called 'Marius'. He probably shouldn't have clicked on it but, well, he did.

The stuff people say about how he looks — he gets it, he honestly gets it, but seeing the thumbnail images there, hundreds of them, on J-P's own screen, had reanimated some of the worst experiences he'd faced as a boy; the mocking whistles, the catcalls on the street — *Olá gatinha!* — interspersed with suggestive or obscene gestures, and even, occasionally, mauling and manhandling.

Small and pretty as he was, guys would genuinely mistake him for a girl, no matter how he dressed. One time — he was maybe twelve and still learning the best response was to do nothing, say nothing — a guy who realised the mistake he'd made, and in front of all his buddies too, flipped out and grabbed at him, pulling him to the ground. *'You smile at me like that, bagulho? I'll cut your tiny balls off.'*

He started working out at sixteen, after his growth spurt had finally happened, making him so skinny the other guys at the gym howled when he started off by lifting the bar only. It wasn't long before he could add some weights, and he took up the kickboxing too, on a fast track to turning semi-pro. If ever anyone threatened to cut off his balls again, he'd have to be ready to face them down.

And though he worked hard to build himself up over the subsequent years, to reinforce and steel himself, structural weaknesses remain. Paradoxically, he's turned himself into someone looked at by countless millions, the body he created and face he was lucky enough to be born with, inescapably public, but he's begun to hate straight-acting more than the fear that formed him.

J-P's predilection for the different aromas and various flavours of his body reminds him of the sexiness that permeated the gym, the boxing ring — the sight and smell of men, the grunting feel of them, could be overwhelming — and he happily played along. What confuses him about all those photos is that this is what's absent from them.

If people knew how he thinks about himself they'd hardly credit it. He'd run away from his femme self by taking that part of him into the most macho arena imaginable, but he has never dealt with the fucked-up-self-hating-scared-gay-boy terror he buried somewhere back home, but which still calls out to him like a ghost in the night.

It was Leslie Cheung who told him once, "Marius, we all grow up in fear, but once you let go of that, well, it can transform your life. Do you know what's most tragic? The thing you're most afraid of, is you." He misses poor Leslie; so adored, so wise with others, and so unhappy, hurling his body into the night sky like that.

Only three months ago, he and J-P had gone to the Metropolitan Museum together. He knew those paintings meant so much to J-P and, following him up the grand staircase, treading the galleries in nervous silence, he'd thought, What if I don't like them? What if I don't feel anything?

They'd entered the Cézanne room and he'd actually exhaled an *Oh!* in front of the still life with apples and primroses and was immediately wrapped up in the painting's blue-green brightness, had been moved, genuinely, by the crimson and green apples and the orange ones that could almost be oranges, beside the pale pink flowers.

Motivated by that green-blue background, the apples, and those primroses especially, whose leaf stalks stretched out like wide-open arms, waiting to embrace them both, he'd gone to J-P, who was sitting on the bench in the middle of the room, whispered the single word, "*Astonishing*," into his ear and put a hand on his knee, but only briefly because some asshole had already snapped a picture.

What does this all mean, now, for them? What's happened has made any future impossible, whatever way you look at it. He could speak. He could ask J-P, *Which of those portraits is the real me? Tell me who you think I am?*

They could have a conversation about how fucked up the whole situation is, help each other out. But he doesn't know how to play that scene, what lines to speak, and neither could he improvise it. Say nothing, do nothing, he repeated, in time to his breathing.

When he'd bounded into J-P's trailer just now, and into his arms, he wasn't acting but it took only a few seconds to remember what he'd gone through in his mind last night — *What's the best way to play this?* — until J-P had returned from his dinner with Maria and he'd pretended to be asleep. Do nothing, say nothing.

He suddenly pictures himself picking up J-P's laptop and bringing it down on the table where it sits in front of him right now, smashing it and everything around them into fragments of glass. This vision has the same energy as when he'd played Paul taking up his palette knife, piling it with paint, attacking his canvas; smearing, pressing, stabbing the surface, to creating the new, horrifying surface of *The Murder*.

So much frustration and rage in him, and in Paul. He'll use it. But he wants merely to be an apple, nestled in the folds of a crumpled cloth, given shelter and protection by the outstretched leaves of a pot of primroses.

He reaches out for that, breathes towards that and feels there is something there, in his hand. He opens his eyes and looks down to see J-P's hand there, resting in his own.

"Time to go," J-P says.

Sophie, New York — 2006

Slouched on the gallery's bench, opposite Hortense, Sophie lacked the guts to do what she really wanted, which was to speak all her thoughts aloud; about last night's exhibit opening, about Christa's call that had come this morning while she was towelling herself dry and what it meant for her future, and how she had a date in a few hours with some cute guy. *A poet, Hortense!*

No, she wasn't going to be one of those crazies who sit in the Metropolitan Museum talking to the pictures, not yet, anyway, but she and Hortense had always been able to commune silently, mind to mind and it was right to come see her after yesterday. There was no one else she'd rather share her news with, nowhere else she'd rather be than the Met's Cézanne rooms, where each painting made a story of its own and, gathered in this space, coalesced into some larger thing.

She spun herself slowly round on the smooth wooden bench, which was like travelling through Cézanne's nervous system, or scanning his consciousness.

There were apples, of course, always the apples, and fruit stands and dishes, netted eggplants hanging from a hook, tables and flowers and fabric.

Then there was one of his obsessive renderings of *Mont Sainte-Victoire*, alongside the airy, light-filled seaside landscape around L'Estaque.

The darkly menacing, tree-lined paths of the Jas de Bouffin, the country estate Cézanne had inherited after his father's death.

Men seated around a table, played cards and smoked their pipes, and solitary men in armchairs, staring out into the middle distance.

There was also a strange, vivid portrait of Cézanne's uncle wearing what looked like a relaxed, yellow bathrobe over his suit, with some kind of collapsed nightcap on his head, its black silk tassel — as deeply black as his suit, as black as his beard and his eyes — dangling beside his ear.

But it was the portraits of Hortense, Cézanne's wife, that never failed to enthral Sophie. She'd written her MFA thesis on them, trying to figure out the whole time what it was she loved about them — love at first sight, actually.

One of them, *Madame Cézanne in the Conservatory*, showed Hortense dressed in midnight blue and sitting beside dusky pink flowers, her head tilted to one side, her pretty face quizzical and sad. Like the *Mont Sainte-Victoire*, it was unfinished. Inside its rough squiggles and areas of exposed canvas Hortense appeared composed, relaxed, perhaps on the verge of asking a question.

It was this Hortense with whom she usually communed but, today, the other Hortense had beckoned her over the minute she got there. Though she had the same chestnut-coloured hair, parted in the middle and fastened at the back, and the same rosy cheeks, she was sitting stiffly upright beside a fireplace, her bold red dress tied loosely at the collar and cinched in at the waist. Her long, oval face was a mask; eyes blank, nose straight, mouth set firmly in anxious resignation.

The blue drawing room she inhabited was one of her husband's experiments in colour and multiple perspectives; its angles, lines and corners all off kilter, the high-backed, yellow armchair about to fall over, tipping Hortense into a heavily swagged floral curtain. Looking at her, Sophie was transported back to the vivid sensation of this morning's dream and had to grip the bench to stop herself from tipping off it, likewise.

In it, she was descending the Met's wide stone staircase, stepping cautiously because her body was made of thin crystal, bending the light, distorting the lines of the stairs, the walls, as she moved. She'd stopped to examine a painting, extravagantly framed in ornate gilt wood, a portrait of herself, her naked body all smooth and pudgy in the neo-Classical style, lifting a glass arm to view the picture through it. Her glossy painted flesh had bulged and spread before her glass eyes. How had she come to be so transformed?

She'd turned away, then, frightened, and lost her balance, was launched into the air, the world rippling as she flew through it. She held her breath until the startling moment she hit the stone floor and was smashed into glass fragments, which was the moment she blinked awake, the tinkling of her shattering body and the tinkling ringtone of her Blackberry one and the same.

What was that all about exactly? She was feeling breakable, obviously. That'd be right. It was already one of the most significant days of her life and she couldn't just enjoy this moment, oh no, she had to imagine herself smashed to smithereens. Maybe this Hortense, squashed and skewed in a corner, posing reluctantly at the insistence of her genius husband, was what she was all about today.

There'd been maybe a half second or so after waking of feeling okay, before the steel clip behind her eyes clenched shut and her stomach flipped over. She was in for quite the hangover.

She'd thought it was Christa calling, to give her the night's gossip, so had picked up with a croaky "Hey," but it wasn't Christa, it was this guy talking. She looked at the unknown number on the screen, then put it back to her ear in time to hear something about "Caffe Reggio, tiramisu," and knew then it was poet guy.

"Great," she heard, "great," and he'd sounded out of breath, as if he'd run to the phone, but no, he'd called her, at — what time? — almost midday by then she saw, looking at the screen once more. "So that's good for you?" he asked. He had not yet stopped speaking.

"I'm sorry," she'd begun, with a dry laugh, "could you say that again? I'm a bit out of it this morning."

"Oh, God, sorry. Did I wake you?

"No, no. I was awake, just not. You know. *Up.*"

"I'm sorry. Course. Last night was a big night for you, right?"

"It might have been," she'd said. "I'm not sure."

He suggested meeting at eight, but that was too late for her — "I'm gonna need an early night," — and said six instead, which was no problem for him. "And — sorry — it's Joel, right?" She'd been quite certain that was his name but ought to be sure.

There'd been a pause before he said, "Yeah, Joel. And you're Sophie Number One."

So he'd seen them, her pictures, of course he had. How could he not have? "Yes, that's me. Sophie Number One."

He'd wished her a great day then and she was relieved they weren't going to talk more at that point — it was probably for the best. He must have been relieved it was over, poor guy. She'd optimistically saved his contact after that, then hauled her ass into the shower, to rinse herself from the inside out, scrub her crystal body squeaky clean.

She caught herself, now, biting at the corner of her thumbnail, and stopped with an inward admonishment. She'd made herself bleed a little and licked the red raw skin. Hortense's hands, resting in her lap, were holding a flower that was unidentifiable being just a mass of squiggles, and culminated in worried, confused fingers. In the other painting, the fingers were sketched out only, in anxious, dark blue lines that matched her dress.

These unfinished workings out seemed to expose the fact that Cézanne knew his wife's face — could vary and experiment with its planes and facets — but not her hands. It was like he was frightened of them. In each case, Sophie thought, he'd silenced her by drawing a mouth so tightly closed it would require monumental effort to speak. Except she wasn't silent. Despite her husband's best attempt, Hortense did speak to Sophie — about herself, about them both, and about the man she sat for, the husband who painted her. His anxiety had become her anxiety, his worried hands, *her* worried hands. They were portraits of Cézanne as much as of her. It wasn't Hortense who was so different and the same in these paintings, it was him.

She took from her shoulder bag the slender book she always brought here with her and made a note of this thought in one of its margins. Annie Yeung's study of Cézanne, *Shadow is a Colour as Light is*, wasn't your standard art history but a sort of personal diary of looking; tentative and delicate, Yeung was trying to get at something in Cézanne, and in Hortense too, while being aware she might not succeed.

Like Hortense, the book spoke to Sophie in ways she didn't fully understand, its messages coded and cloudy. Sophie used Annie Yeung as a model when writing her thesis, combining academic conventions with her personal observation, but worried that she'd still turned Hortense into a mere subject, squashed her into a corner like her husband.

She carried Cézanne's full quotation around with her, in her head, and recited it to herself sometimes like a mantra — *shadow is a colour as light is, but less brilliant; light and shadow are only the relation of two tones.* It made her think of her life as well as anything about painting, or her own portraits.

She had shadows of her own, inside and out, and her art was a bringing forward of light and colour that only served to deepen the shadows and the relation between the two. She didn't fully understand what all this meant yet, maybe never would, but the sense of it thrilled her because a lifetime's work was potentially contained in lucid thoughts like these, questions that were simple but large. She'd gotten used to waiting for fragments of answers, knowing full well she might never get to construct their entirety.

Having initially struggled to settle on an idea for her final MFA show — the works that Christa had seen and then offered to include in her first group exhibit — Sophie had decided she would become her own subject. The self-portrait would form the basis of her practice, for the time being. Her research, her looking at Hortense over and over, had brought her to the firm position that no one would but herself would ever paint her and that she would do it openly, free from anxiety, which was not at all how she felt. Sophie's decision to be naked in her self-portraits was hers alone and her use of colour transformed her body into something else, though certainly not fragile crystal glass to be smashed on the floor of a museum.

All she knew was that she wanted to consider herself from the point of view of object and subject together, to control the way she was seen but also to try to figure out who she was in the act of painting; like Cézanne trying to figure out what the apple was, or the mountain, or his wife; like Annie Yeung had been trying to figure out who she was, Sophie felt, in the conjoined acts of looking and writing about looking.

Last night, Christa had told her that this Joel, the poet guy, was 'complex', which could mean anything. She'd also mentioned they had a 'thing' once; 'brief and messy', she'd called it. "He has this game he plays — if he asks you to come up with a subject for a poem, just say anything, whatever comes into your head…"

Sophie was about to ask Christa why it hadn't worked out between them when he'd come on over. Though she suspected Christa wasn't exactly a walk in the park either. No, that was unfair, Christa was great. She'd been drunk enough to just go with it, but sober enough to have the presence of mind to mask her alarm at her internal reaction to inky-assed poet guy — a kind of involuntary *Shazam!* — who was not handsome exactly, more intensely ordinary looking, with a wounded quality, evidenced by the permanently questioning brow and nervy jiggling, which, God forgive her, Sophie was drawn to.

Then, when she and Christa spoke earlier today, of course she'd been too bowled over to ask her anything about Joel and his ink-stained ass, and then too embarrassed to disclose that she'd arranged to meet up with him this very evening, which was why they couldn't go have a celebration drink together. Instead, she'd claimed tiredness and a headache, which wasn't a lie exactly because she was still fuzzy with both.

She's really not sure about the whole thing. As much as she didn't want anyone else to paint her ever, she didn't want to be written about either. Muses were unreal, trapped in frames, and it didn't matter whether those were gilded or poetic.

The whole writing-her-number-on-his-hand incident flashed across her vision and she felt herself blushing, pictured her own cheeks as pink as those on Hortense's face, whose two painted expressions — the quizzical and tender, the stern and anxious — directed themselves at Sophie both at once.

"I know I know I know," she whispered. "Stupid, right?"

Abrupt, noisy squawks of rubber-soled sneakers against the wooden

111

floor made her turn towards a hefty guy striding into the room, making a racket so intrusive that everyone in the space shifted their gaze to him. He halted directly in front of Cézanne's apples and flowers, lifted the large, menacing camera hanging from a strap round his neck, took a second — maybe a second and a half — to point, focus, click, before stomping across the room and out the other doorway, his sneaker's squeals and squeaks echoing through the space.

"Can you believe that?" Sophie demanded to no one in particular. "He barely looked! Just wanted to snap an image on his fucking memory card — or whatever — not his actual memory. That's how it'll always look for him now, because he never actually saw it. *Ach!*"

She raised her arms in exasperation and tossed her book into her bag, slung it over her shoulder and stood up, all in one action, though too fast because the steel clip that had been in abeyance up until then, clamped down hard on her optic nerve.

Sophie managed to wave a sort of goodbye to Hortense, which set her to swaying, but she managed to rush out of the room in one piece, clench receding. She should cancel this date thing and go on home, that's what she should do, but, just then, she heard Hortense calling out: "Say yes! Today is a day for saying yes!"

Caffe Reggio's green-painted front, normally so pretty, was nauseating today. Through the windows she could see the space was busy, but there was no way to make out if he was inside, or not.

A woman exiting, on seeing Sophie hovering there, held the door open for her. She felt she had no choice then but to enter the darkly cramped interior and saw him immediately, sitting at the table by the payphone, the one inside its own booth with the bust of Nefertiti on a shelf above your head.

She wove her way through the room, shrugging off the favourite soft, red leather jacket that she wore to keep herself together, and when he stood up to usher her past him into the booth, the weird *Shazam!* thing happened again. He was wearing jeans, but these had no ink-blot at the ass, she noticed. It was, no doubt about it, a great ass.

As she put down her bag, adjusted the shoulder straps on her navy blue summer dress, tucked her hair behind her ear, her hands fluttered like birds conjured from her sleeves before she was quite ready for them.

"Well, this is my *favourite* spot," she declared, to the whole place it felt like, as if he had executed a major coup to secure, for their first date, the most sought after table in the whole of New York. She was over-compensating and annoyed at herself for it. She needed to calm the fuck down.

"I got you a present," was the next thing she said. He appeared startled and she smiled a brittle glass smile.

They fell silent as the waitress placed menus in front of them, while Sophie rifled through her bag and took out a slim cardboard slipcase. She placed it on the table between them. It was a box of pencils, red ones, with *Metropolitan Museum of Art* stamped along them in gold.

"I just came from there," she said, "and I saw these in the gift shop and thought they'd be the *perfect* thing for you. Y'know, to stop your ass from getting all inky. Though I notice that's not a problem today."

She'd meant it to sound all light and playful but ended up poking fun at him before he'd hardly said a word. His eyebrows danced nervously and there was that questioning forehead she remembered.

"Well," he managed, "thank you. I was planning on getting some pencils myself but now I needn't bother. I'm really, really glad to have these, which are just so," — he picked up the box and waved it in the air like a magic wand — "elegant."

The waitress came back, thank God, and, at Joel's insistence, Sophie ordered for them both. "Two tiramisu and some green tea. Please." She sat back and sighed. "Perfect."

"Last night was really something, wasn't it?"

"It was. It really was."

"And your paintings, well, they were incredible."

"Oh. Thank you. Really?"

"Sure. I can't imagine what it must feel like to put yourself on the line like that. I mean, to really show yourself in that way. I think it's very brave. And the colours. *Amazing* colours. Truly."

"To be honest, I don't feel at all brave about it. It's like it's me and it's not me. It's painting. I look at myself so much when I'm doing it that I'm not me anymore. Like when you say a word over and over so many times it sounds alien."

"So you don't feel exposed? Even though you're naked?"

"Oh, I feel exposed, sure, but no one could scrutinise me as much as I've scrutinised myself in the making of those pictures, so I get a certain, kind of, I don't know, *power* from that. No, it's not power, exactly. Strength. I'm not saying I don't care what people think about the paintings. I do. A lot. But I don't care what they think about me — my body, my ego, whatever." She did care, though, about what he might think of what she'd just said about her work, and herself, wrestled with the impulse to retract or apologise somehow. But this was something that, as an artist and a woman, she'd resolved to stop doing.

He was tracing the outline of the box of pencils with his fingers, nodding gently. She should ask him about his work but fought that impulse too. They could talk about her a little longer, couldn't they?

"And that guy?" he said, without looking at her, "the one they were all taking photos of? Who was that?"

"Well, it's kind of incredible really. He's some hot young movie actor who I've not heard of — well, I've *heard* of him but not seen anything he's done. Christa invited him to the show because apparently he's made truckloads of money and is looking to become a collector. And, well, he bought my work. *All* of it. Can you believe that? Christa called me this morning, right after I spoke to you."

He looked at her now, delighted. "Oh my God, that's great!"

"I know, right? I can hardly believe it. I mean, I'm nobody and these paintings, well, you saw them... I'm still working out what my work is all about, but I guess he liked them and you have to start somewhere."

"We should totally celebrate."

"Y'know, you're right, we should. I've been nursing a hangover all day but now I can feel it lifting."

He nodded to the waitress: "Can we get two glasses of Prosecco? Is that okay?" he asked her. "Prosecco?"

Sophie nodded. "You're only the second person I've told," she said.

"The second!" he exclaimed, mock-offended. "Who was the first?"

"Oh — " she couldn't tell him it was the long suffering, long dead wife of Paul Cézanne — "Sorry, I mean you're only the second person who knows. After Christa."

The drinks arrived then, Prosecco and tea all together, along with the tiramisu. They both sat back and admired the sheer beauty of the gently graded layers of dark brown bleeding into creamy white. It had come in small, cut-crystal bowls and Sophie wanted to hold on tight to hers, to prevent it shattering.

"I hope you're making a mental note of this," she said, "for my poem. I haven't forgotten."

"Me neither."

Sophie lifted the Prosecco to him. "Cheers," she said, and he raised his glass in salute. The sweet fizz was delicious.

She felt strangely calm, anticipating the hit of coffee and dry cocoa and mascarpone as she picked up her spoon; it really was perfect. "I haven't eaten all day," she said.

"Me neither."

She laughed. "I'm gonna totally destroy this."

"Me too."

Paul, Paris — 1868

He had thought to see Émile tomorrow but his friend's note insisted he couldn't wait another moment, not now he knew of Paul's return. Pulling his greatcoat tight around him he shivers uneasily. It must be the damp from the river. The city is unusually, damnably, cold, though not like the Provençal cold that braces and cleanses the body from the inside out. How he misses it. He should be out walking in the forest, tasting the sharp, green air, bathing in the fresh green waters.

"The light here is no good!" he declaims, to no one but himself. It doesn't have the dazzling blue-white brilliance of the sky at Aix. Nor is he truly inspired here as he is by the depth and variety he perceives in the mountain and the trees, in the hills and deep valleys and the small towns tucked in the folds between.

How quickly his excitement for Paris wanes. No patience for the daubers and their disciples, the time-wasting café-dwellers. "Shithead *fools*, all of them." Passers-by look at him askance at the best of times, even more so when he curses into the air like this. He hates them all the more for it.

Like those two women there, across the boulevard, staring and laughing at him, mimicking his upward gaze with a mocking intensity,

117

he's sure of it, but he doesn't care. "Imbeciles!" strutting up and down but going nowhere, he wants nothing to do with them. Yet… he cares what they think. But *why* does he?

The more he cares, the more he craves the countryside and the freedom to paint, as a caged animal craves the freedom to roam and hunt. He will stalk the hostile streets on the way to join Émile, all the while imagining he inhabits the beloved landscape of their youth.

There is, perhaps, rain coming. This morning he'd woken into thin, early spring light but the sky was clouding over. It was usually his favourite time in the studio, but he'd felt so listless, lying there on the divan, and felt the half-finished canvas that sat on the easel summoning him.

Realising his nightshirt had twisted round his body during the night, and was restraining him like a shroud, he had pulled himself up, torn the shirt off and kicked his way through the oily rags and dirty palettes covering the floor (he sent a paintbrush, sticking to his foot, clattering into a corner) to fling open the window and gulp for air. His exposed flesh had tightened and goose-pimpled — as it did when he and Émile plunged into the ponds after one of their long treks — and the accompanying contraction in his groin awakened the memory of the morning's dream-vision, pulling to the surface his desire for the model who had lain the day before on the very same divan where he slept. Some of her scent must have remained there, like an infection.

Heavy-limbed, with delicate hands and feet, her corn-gold hair and clotted cream skin had emitted an astonishingly radiant glow. Her breasts were small and rose-tipped, and her pudenda shone dark pink and violet beneath her pale, abundant, bush. He barely spoke to her beyond giving brusque instructions and, when she'd gone (after accepting her payment with a bold, straightforward look to which he did not respond), he'd paced the room, furious.

Then, in the sleepy dawn, he'd felt her climb on top and straddle him, her delicate hands now clawing, tearing, trying to get inside his very flesh. But he won't be distracted from his art, which is his life. He has seen it happen to so many of his friends, try as they might to prevent it. But hadn't he, in truth, wanted her?

A bombardment of horses' hooves clattering on the cobbles behind pulls him from his agitated reverie to be once again surrounded by the terrible clamour of wagons and carriages and bustling people. The light of the morning has been totally subsumed now by thin grey cloud, like cheap gauze laid over the sky — "*Ach!*" — he can't bear it. The wafting hot hay smell of the horses, that, at least, he loves. Surely there is a way to make this city work for him? It is the centre of the world, after all. But, oh, for the simple joy of wolfing down a fresh omelette cooked on the campfire after a long trek and invigorating bathe… He cannot recapture such pleasures here.

Before Paul came to Paris, Émile had filled his letters with stories of who he'd met and what he'd seen — the parties, the painters, the writers, the women — and his excitement had been contagious, but it was not Paul's excitement and never could be. He mutters, "Must we meet today?" It requires so much effort he is weary merely thinking of it.

He trudges on. His appearance will only embarrass Émile, as will his refusal to indulge in idiotic café chitchat. He would rather confine himself to his studio and never leave it (always he must fight this impulse). He shakes his head vehemently, flicking words and thoughts from his mind "Yes!" he barks into the sky, they must meet.

Paul must enter the café where they will all be, and the volume of chatter will dim momentarily. He must stand there, shuffling, as they take in his dishevelled country garb of smelly coat, wool trousers and boots, his unkempt hair poking out from beneath his felt hat. They will recoil from his outstretched hands streaked with paint and he will enjoy that. "Why should I wash them?" Why wash away the signs of work? "God knows how fucking hard it is!"

A man — some *popinjay* — drawing alongside him in the opposite direction stops dead, abashed, and Paul squawks in his face — *"Ha! Ha! Ha!"* — with a flash of delight, just as he'd enjoyed deliberately grasping Manet's hands with his filthy paws that time, all but ruining the beautiful, pale-yellow kid leather gloves he was wearing. He will be there no doubt, with all his hangers-on in attendance, but Paul won't play the fawning game.

Exhausted suddenly, weighted down, he stops and rubs his forehead, his eyes. He shouldn't torture himself like this - it would be better if Manet liked him – no, he doesn't care! "They can all eat shit!" He does care.

He'll see Émile, drink a brandy or two with him and endeavour not to embarrass his friend, or anyone else, and least of all himself. Even if he were to ignore his note and return now to his lodging, Émile would simply visit and Paul doesn't want him floating around, struggling to compliment his work, pretending not to notice the squalor.

Things have changed between them, there is no doubt. They were going to devour the whole world. They had left behind their boyhood selves, for whom everything was at stake and anything was possible. When arguments were enjoyed and forgotten in a moment, and they didn't disappoint each other. Where did all the tenderness go? Émile used to calm him; now, he is most angry at Émile.

Paris does, occasionally, give Paul what he had hoped for; its incomparable variety of people, the capacity to absorb, reflect, magnify life's infinite experience, engaging all the senses at once. But his devastation at the realisation that this same city was determined to spurn him at every opportunity — the Salon, the École, the other artists, the fetid models who wrinkle their noses at him — has been utterly crushing. He can't do anything here. "Can't *paint*. Can't *think*." It is the capital of the world, and he hates it.

They had imagined, he and the other Inseparables he means, that Paris would cure him of his discontent, but it has only made things worse. All the activities his friends take pleasure in — drinking, smoking, talking, whoring — are no use to him. Instead, everything irritates and angers and Émile blames Paul, not Paris, for his profound unhappiness. The city, his family, his friends — all fail to live up to his grand ideals. And he too fails. He has uncovered here a many-layered and terrifying disquiet deep inside worse than anything the world may throw at him.

As long as he remains here, he will never pull himself free.

He could drop down now, in the street, depleted.

Then, the colours of something in a shop window beside him — a hat — *a hat*, of all things! — arrests him. Its smooth green velvet, dark as a wine bottle, fringed with pale, primrose pink and a ribbon of clear-sky-blue sings out through the glass. "Those colours!" So alive… It is undoubtedly those colours that prevented his collapse. There are so many possibilities in the world, if he could only manage life.

He isn't happy here but he isn't truly happy in Aix either, he must admit that. At least here he doesn't have Old Father Cézanne looking over his shoulder, trying to pressgang him, as always, into the law.

Paul has tried to do what his father wants — moving back home, following his legal studies, relegating drawing and painting to a hobby — all to please him, all because his father doesn't understand the pull of painting that returns to the fore no matter how hard he tries to resist it.

He loves and hates all at once; the frustration, the listlessness, the desperate energy, the feeling worthless, alongside the certain knowledge that, out of all of them, he is the best, the most original genius.

He moves closer to the milliner's window, flooding his field of vision with the blue-green of the hat display's backdrop, chosen to intensify the shimmering bottle green, the blue ribbon, the soft blushing pink. He sees, then, the model's dark pink places, rests his forehead against the glass to support and cool himself.

Paul would rather live as a pauper here than do his father's bidding back there. Even now, having given Paul permission once more to study in Paris, he keeps his son on a short financial leash. His insistence that Paul make money from his art, that he must enrol at the École or return home, that the Salon must accept him before he, his own father, can accept him, drives him to despair. As if any of that means anything apart from the opportunity for the old man, a petty bourgeois who understands nothing, to boast of what a great success his son is.

"It's impossible. Impossible. I can't…"

He pulls his head away from the glass, sees the dim reflection of his own lips moving, and the heat rises again in his face. He has fogged a patch of the window with his breathy mutterings and wipes them away with the sleeve of his coat.

At the clear sight of himself he yelps a laugh. He is monstrous, it has to be said; his features massive, his long, black hair already thinning, though his anarchist's beard is luxurious still, his beetle-brow truly terrifying if you have no sense, no idea, of what it means to struggle as he does, if you do not know the person trapped within.

Will he tart himself up like a simpleton to please the Academy idiots? "No."

Rent himself out to indulge the vanity of those complacent bourgeois *bastards*, who want their portraits painted? "No!"

Émile knows all that is required to make a name for yourself. They were going to take Paris by the scruff of the neck and shake it, hard — but they hadn't understood what that meant. These days, Émile has grown more handsome, urbane even. Women like him too, flocking to him even more since the great success *de scandale of Thérèse Raquin*, while Paul barely has the guts to even look at a woman outside of the studio, let alone speak to one. How different they are from the sensuous maids they dreamed about as they wandered through Aix, how different is the reality from that pure and noble love they once craved.

Émile has become the kind of man who would have an opinion about these hats in the window, a conversation about them even. There's a rumour that he sits for Manet now, that Manet is painting his portrait.

Émile will succeed because he's prepared to play them at their own game. But Paul will not. "They deserve each other," he mutters, grimly.

No, he's being disloyal, unworthy of his dearest friend who has helped him so much — even interceding with the Old Man on Paul's behalf, just as when they'd fought the bullies together at school (he can hear the laughter of boys somewhere) — and Paul loves him immensely for it, the big brother he had wished for, always the first to defend him, even here in Paris.

It is Émile, and only Émile, who has encouraged him, who has helped give him his new life in Paris, for better or worse, and only he who truly understands what it means for Paul to be Paul. "Émile, Émile, Émile…" They were, and surely still are, Inseparables.

His focus shifts and brings to his attention a group of ragamuffin boys reflected on the pavement behind him — it was they who were laughing just now — real laughter, not his memory's malicious recollection. How long have they been watching him? What have they witnessed, or heard him say?

He thrusts his hands in his pockets, feels the squat, encrusted blade of the little palette knife he'd forgotten was there, pulls it out to look at

123

it. A flake of dried, blue-black paint drops onto his boot. He grips the knife's smooth wooden handle with his growing anger, then spins round to brandish it at the gang. "Fuck off you little shit-eaters," he growls.

The boys jump back as one, then "*Ooooh*," jeeringly.

Paul turns back to the window display. If he ignores them they will go away. In the glass, he sees, too late, one of them scoop a clot of half-dried dung from the roadside and throw it. Before he can dodge aside the horseshit strikes his backside with a dull thump.

"*You* eat shit!" the boy catcalls and the whole gang cackles and hoots and scampers away.

Paul flashes hot and dizzy. He feels himself tumbling, tumbling, sees stairs and feet and floor. How long, how long, he has worked to forget the traumas of childhood, and yet back there he is, in less than an instant, falling, falling.

He places a hand against the window to prevent himself crashing through the glass. He can hardly breathe, sinks, slumps to sitting.

In the distance the boys jostle each other, pushing and shoving, punching, kicking, laughing. It's so easy for them — being alive — why is it not easy for him? How is life to be borne? How is it to be tolerated?

He could take the palette knife still in his tight fist and plunge it into his own eyes, his heart, crusted paint and all. He clambers to his feet. He will go back home. He will do the only thing he can at moments like these, which is to paint.

Breath easing, his focus rests on a woman across the street, peering quizzically at the grubby lunatic who speaks into the window of a hat shop, a grown man who is assaulted by children in the street then flops down onto the ground like the piece of shit he is.

She looks away when he meets her gaze but does not yet walk on.

Paul thinks she wants to examine the hat shop's display, but is afraid to approach while he is blocking it. He can just make out the delicate, pearly shell of one ear — the same pale pink of the fringing on that hat, he sees — and a wisp of hair that has come loose.

He envisions himself standing behind her, placing his hands on her waist. He quivers at the imagined touch of her on his dirty palms, feels her yielding to him, leaning into his body, the line of him shaping the line of her. In life there are no outlines, he thinks, just shapes, colours, light and shadow, and shadow *is* a colour, as light is.

She glances across once more and he sees her more clearly. Her face is not beautiful but is infused with intelligence, curiosity and, he thinks, kindness. Could such a woman like him?

No one of any value would think him attractive. Even those tarts who offer themselves round to all his fellow artists have given up on him,. They consider him brutish, a barbarian. The model who silently offered herself yesterday to him must have been desperate for the extra money.

Is he never to know the intimate touch of a woman? Never to kiss, to stroke, to fuck, to feel? He should have paid the price, and taken her.

He will speak to this woman, instead. He will tell her he is not a vagrant, nor a madman.

As he strides boldly across, a maelstrom of emotions and sensations flickers across her face: surprise, embarrassment, fear, revulsion, pity, amusement; he sees them all before she collects herself and makes off down the street.

From the side, her figure, swathed in dove grey silk shot with lavender, only increases his desire — her breasts not too full, her belly slightly rounded, and her hands, her hands that flutter about as she struggles to pull on her gloves, have long, fine fingers.

He follows, powered by the urge to explain that he is only a great, unhappy painter. Could he take hold of her? Force her hand into his?

He would only sully it. The filthy mitts that amused him before distress him now. But still, these stained hands, along with the paint-encrusted knife, are proof of who he truly is. He must make her *see* that.

Thrusting the blade before him, he lurches faster, is drawn into the wake of her perfume, a floral mix of primroses and lilac and it halts him. What is he doing?

A voice calls out — "Paul!" — it is Émile's voice, but when he searches all around and above him, Émile is not there.

Something about the sky terrifies him, filled as it is now with storm clouds, roiling like the sea, pressing down, pressing, pressing....

He reaches up with the palette knife as if to puncture the sky's violent mass, to let the air out and a vision comes; a painting of that sky, the retreating woman's dark blonde hair, loose, trailing on the ground, a knife, a boot planted firmly — his boot — another woman — the model — complicit in death — the horror of now.

This is the kind of reality he must create; a true reality, a terrible reality. If Émile can do it so can he.

He pushes the knife into his pocket, turns to go back to where he belongs; standing in front of the easel, facing his canvas and the questions of painting.

"Émile will have to wait."

Maria, Liverpool — 2008

Maria rushes into the Walker, late she knows and worried by how Nick will be. She stops at the sight of him hunched over paper, drawing, the back of his neck looking exactly the same as the boy's of fifteen who, on that morning when she'd heard about his dad and gone round straightaway and opened the back door that was never locked and seen Nick sat at in the kitchen with a pile of broken eggshells on the table in front of him, drawing them with this crackling fury, like he couldn't not do it.

Sue, Nick's mum, was standing at the hob and neither of them noticed Maria when she walked in. Then Sue had looked up as she plopped a glistening, freshly fried egg on a plate warming on the top of the grill, underneath which some rashers of bacon were spitting gently. "Hello, Maria love," she said, like she always did, and Maria hugged her, though only for a second because Sue turned straight back to the stove, spatula in hand.

"I heard what happened," Maria said.

"Where'd you hear exactly?" Nick asked from the table, without looking up.

"It's all over the place," Maria told him, but she didn't say it was even on the local news that morning. "I'm — I'm really sorry. I don't know what else to say. Poor Jimmy."

She'd sat down across from Nick and reached over and placed her hand on his, the one that was resting on the edge of the paper to keep it straight.

Sue cracked another egg into the pan and its sizzling filled the silence. She reached across, added the newly halved shells to the pile in front of Nick and his thin sketch of them.

Thinking about it now, Maria wasn't surprised that Nick and his mum were acting so normal, in spite of what had happened, because that was how they lived their lives; acting normal in the face of horrendous violence. She'd not asked Nick then, and has never asked since, why he hadn't phoned her himself. She'd been frightened of the answer he might give, of making him angry for making it about her — that was one of his common accusations in those days.

She'd been frightened of his reactions to things for as long as she could remember and she mustn't be frightened now — though she is — at the sight of him sitting head bowed in the café of the Walker, drawing, which had come to indicate different things at different times in their lives, until it was impossible to read what it meant, inside their relationship. Eventually, Maria had stopped encouraging him, stopped asking, "How's your art going?" because it could spark a sulk, a storming out, a row, sex, she could never be sure. It was manic, that's what it was. Drawing was the only mind-altering substance Nick had used — before his medication, she means. The highs were amazing. He was such a joy to be with then. But the comedowns, the times it wasn't going right, they were just awful.

What she'd heard that terrible morning, seeing something wrong on her mum's face when she'd brought her a cup of tea in bed, which she never did, was, "Jimmy's really gone and done it now."

Maria had never seen her mum so angry and so controlled at the same time, remembers that the cup and saucer jangled with it, and Maria's first thought was Nick, he's killed Nick, but he hadn't, her mum said, "he's only gone and ruined the rest of his bloody life for him," which was almost as bad.

And her mum told Maria what Maria's dad told her when he came back from the pub last night; that there'd been a lock-in but Jimmy hadn't stayed for it, had left when the guitar and the fiddle came out and the singing started, and the pub door was bolted behind him, and if the curtains hadn't been drawn someone might have seen Jimmy sitting in his car all that time and eventually gone out to him, to check he was alright. Or they might've seen what he was doing with the can of petrol and stopped him, but they hadn't seen anything, and they were singing and playing so loud by then that they didn't hear the whoosh of the fire when it started and she just hoped to God it was quick but it must have been *awful*.

The next thing they knew there was a hammering at the pub door and they all stopped singing because they thought it was the bizzies come about the noise, but it wasn't, it was Nick who'd been sent by Sue to fetch Jimmy back home because she had to be up early the next morning for her shift at the bakery and, despite everything, she never got a proper night's sleep, Sue once told her, unless Jimmy was next to her. "God, she must really have loved him," her mum had said, "and Christ only knows why."

It was Nick who found the car burning with Jimmy inside it, and when they'd all run out the pub to see if what Nick had told them was true, that was when the car windows blew and the flames roared out, and Maria's dad, who hadn't slept a wink, told her there was nothing they could do except call the fire brigade and wait and watch and by God they hoped it was quick. "He's in the bedroom crying to himself now," her mum said, "and don't you tell him I told you that."

And Maria had thought, once a man sets fire to himself, isn't it better to let him burn away if that's what he wants, because to do that to himself he must have really wanted to die so hard that it was best to just let him get on with it, though she'd never said that to Nick.

When Sue put a fried egg butty down in front of her and said, "Have some breakfast won't you love, I'll pour the tea," Maria had started to eat with one hand, all the while keeping the other hand over Nick's while he carried on with his drawing.

She did it for Sue's sake really because she wasn't hungry at all, and the bread turned to cement in her throat, but Sue must have thought people would be calling in to offer condolences and she should give them all fried eggs and bacon butties and cups of tea and, at the same time as Maria realised this, Nick said, "No one will come," and Sue had said, "People *will* come" — spatula flicks quickening — "they'll know *what's right* and they'll come and say sorry and pay your Dad their respects." Then Nick had spat the word, "Respects?" and said, "What are they going to say, Mum? Oh, we're so sorry, Sue. We're sorry your Jimmy's gone and made a show of himself. We're sorry your Nick had to find him burning to death in the car park? We're sorry you don't have to worry about where he is and what he's done ever again? We're sorry the pair of you'll never have to sit in the kitchen waiting for him to come home, listening out for the sound his keys make on the hall table so you can tell whether you're in for a fucking hiding or not and if you're quick enough slip out the back door and walk around for a few hours until he fucking conks out and it's safe to go home?" He'd run out of breath then, Maria remembers, his knuckles whitening around

130

his pencil as he stabbed the table with it, and his hand that was under hers bunching into a fist, screwing up his drawing in the process.

That bunched ball of rage was something that Nick must have buried inside himself because Maria never heard him shout at his mum again after that, because he knew, and his mum and Maria knew, that the person he really wanted to shout at was his dad, but he'd never ever had the guts to do that, and now Jimmy was dead.

Maria takes out her phone to check the exact time and sees she's missed a call from J-P. He'll have to wait.

She takes a big breath to steel herself, tries to calm her heart, *hates* being a liar, but sometimes it's necessary, isn't it? Maybe she should wait until Nick is a bit more settled. No, he'll never be settled. She hates that she thinks about him this way, that he's a burden to her, but it's not her fault. What she worries about most these days is becoming just another angry person in Nick's life, but it's hard always trying to be better. And what are you supposed to do when someone offers you the chance of a lifetime?

She'd already left school at sixteen, hadn't she, to help her mum and dad out with the bills after her dad's redundancy? Not gone to college to do fashion, as she'd wanted, but straight into an admin job with the local council. She thought she might study later, when she'd saved up a bit, but she never did. She'd stayed with Nick because they loved each other since school. In fact, she'd noticed him way before he paid her any attention and they used to laugh about it, how she'd been after him since Primary and he never knew anything about it.

They did everything together; first snog, first sex, first love — in that order. If it had been up to her mum they'd have got married straight after school, but Nick got in to do Fine Art purely on the strength of his portfolio, produced during one of his bouts of stability, and that was amazing given he hadn't done his final exam, so there was no way they could have afforded to get married, and it would have been too soon anyway.

When he'd started hanging out with his arty mates, Nick saw less of her, which was fine because she wanted him to get on and everything, but whenever she was invited to a party or went to an exhibition with them, they'd thought she didn't notice that they talked down to her, glanced at each other then looked away when she'd told them what she thought, gave an opinion. None of them cared that Nick wouldn't even have been there if it wasn't for her; when he'd had his first breakdown at seventeen, and Sue hadn't been able to cope with it, it was Maria who put Nick back together.

All that time she was doing her 'little job' at the Council, as everyone called it, bringing in money, set for life if she wanted, but all she was doing was answering the phone to angry, desperate people, and filing away pieces of paper, or taking files out of cabinets and putting them on other people's desks until eight years had passed and she'd become the person who had files put on her desk and she and Nick were living together after he dropped out of college halfway through.

The day she'd seen the advert in the internal mail for a job in the Film Office her heart had jumped at the thought of doing something like that, even though it was really a demotion to go back to being an administrative assistant, and was less money, but they'd manage and she'd make Nick understand.

Both the interview process and the waiting were agony because she'd wanted it so badly and they'd kind of given her the nod but until it was confirmed she didn't believe it wouldn't be taken away from her. She'd thought what it would mean if she didn't get it, had felt so desperate she hadn't told anyone else she was going for it because she couldn't bear the thought of what she'd say when they gave it to someone else.

But she did get it, and it had her name written all over it that job, felt like her most perfect and best opportunity, right up until the one that was given to her last night.

After only a year, she was made Artist Liaison, a job created specifically for her and which she loved, and then she was taking phone calls from America and Europe, from all over the world, actually, talking to people who could also be desperate and frantic at times because of the deadline pressures they were under and the amounts of money involved, but she knew how to deal with that because it was not that different from the job she had before. She'd been dealing with that all her life it felt like, had to deal with it when she got back home, never knowing what kind of day Nick had had, what mood he was in. Asking him how his day had been was exactly like taking a work call because you never really knew what was going to be on the other end, even though she'd learned to read some of the signals, including the drawing. And all the time, the unspoken thing between them was always Jimmy, because Jimmy possessed him, and so haunted their entire relationship.

At Jimmy's funeral Maria had searched Nick all over for some sign of distress, but his face had stayed flat as a stone, a blank oval, which she supposed was also a sign of his grief, and anger, and hurt, and he barely spoke to anyone that day, met their condolences only with a mute stare.

And Maria had tried really hard to forget the image she had of a burnt and blackened Jimmy that appeared so clear in her mind when she'd watched Nick, and his uncles, and a couple of Jimmy's pub mates carrying his coffin into the church. How light he must be, she'd thought, like charred paper that crumbles when you touch it.

The priest gave a sermon about being plagued by demons and how those demons were made more present by drink, and Maria knew that the men in the church, coughing and shuffling and looking at the floor when he said all that, had already been to the pub beforehand and would all be going there after to give Jimmy a bloody good send-off, treading over the scorch marks in the car park on the way in.

But before that, they went to the crematorium and, as the dark green velvet curtains closed, and the organ music played, Maria had thought, Well they might as well finish what he started.

She'd found herself telling J-P some of this at dinner, last night — not the stuff about Jimmy, just about Nick's depression.

"How come you've been working for the council for so long when you're clearly very bright," J-P had asked, and she'd said, "You can be clever and still work for the council, you know," and they laughed together but she was honestly glad to be asked about herself. She got that J-P liked her speaking to him like a normal person, already like friends after only a few days working together.

She'd asked him about the film, in turn, and J-P had told her about how his dad used to take him to the Walker when his mum was having her treatment in the Royal and there was a painting called *The Murder* by Paul Cézanne, that he'd been frightened of and fascinated by at the same time and how he always used to ask his dad to take him to see it one last time before they left.

Maria had told him that she'd been to the Walker loads of times and seen that picture, though she didn't really like it, but she didn't tell him she'd lobbied really hard to work on this project because she wasn't technically senior enough to coordinate a whole shoot liaison on her own, but she'd used what she remembered from school art classes about Cézanne, dragging up stuff from Paddy all those years ago, stuff she didn't even know she remembered, to convince her boss she should be the one to work with this particular director on this particular project, and, anyway, wasn't it about time they gave her the chance to prove herself?

134

Then J-P told her about how, when he'd gone to the Metropolitan Museum for the very first time, he'd walked into this room which was full of paintings of apples and landscapes and some lovely pictures of his wife who Cézanne didn't really get on with, and he'd started to cry because, ridiculous as it might sound, they were lovely pictures. Then he made it his mission to find out about this artist he remembered from his childhood and how it could be that the same person produced such different paintings from *The Murder*.

He'd told her all about him wanting to astonish Paris with an apple and she didn't say she already knew that story because she loved that J-P was talking to her like an equal and this was what she wanted and she wasn't going to ruin it. And just as she was thinking that J-P said, out of the blue, "Maria, do you fancy coming to work for us?" meaning him and Marius together she'd already guessed, and everything they talked about was leading up to that moment, so she said "Yes," like that, straightaway. She said, "Yes, I'd love that."

But right now, standing in the café of the Walker, watching her ex do the thing that scared her the most, she thought, What if I'm replacing Nick's need of me for J-P's? She knows it's a skill she has — this meeting people's needs — but what about *her*? No, she has to value her skills more — organising, listening to people, being honest with them — because they are skills. It could be a massive stepping-stone for her, this. If it doesn't work out with J-P and Marius she'll move on, work for someone else. She fucking well deserves it. She can't let Nick keep her here forever, that's the truth of it. She has to find out who she is and what she wants because she's hardly ever had the time to think about that. Or she starts to, then stops herself.

But she knows what she doesn't want any more. She's cared for Nick as long as she can remember and she still cares for him, but when he turns and looks up at her now as she approaches the table where he's sitting, it's the same look that he gave her at his mum's kitchen table when she put her hand over his, filled with the same defensive neediness, and even though she loves the boy in him, she doesn't love the man.

She has to move on, she has to, otherwise she'll end up burned alive in a car herself one of these days.

Jeffrey, Hong Kong — 2013

A black carriage trundles briskly over the cobbled Paris street. Suddenly, an arm reaches out the cab window and the driver pulls up sharply. His glossy, chestnut brown horse tosses and shakes its startled head.

Cézanne, muttering darkly, pulling his greatcoat around him, stalks the façade of a grandly imposing edifice. To him, the building's columns are as good as prison bars.

The carriage's cab door swings open and Zola jumps from it, removing his hat with a sweeping gesture. "Paul!" he cries, his round, bearded face blooming into a warm smile.

Cézanne halts, lifts his head, as intensely agitated as the horse.

Zola rushes towards him, arms wide open.

Cézanne's scowl softens and he pulls his hands from his coat pockets.

"So it's true!" Zola exclaims, holding his dear friend by the shoulders. He plants a delighted kiss on Cézanne's scruffy cheek and then the other, pulls him into a hug. "You're really back with us. In Paris."

Cézanne's hands, his long, intelligent fingers crusted with paint, flutter awkwardly around Zola's back before settling into their embrace.

Jeffrey pauses the action, freezing the men in mid hug. He's always liked this scene because of how fragile and humane Cézanne appears.

He can't imagine things would really have happened this way — their physical closeness he means. They show, in the movie, when Hortense touches him for the first time and he flinches, violently, like she's assaulted him. There's a flashback to Cézanne being kicked down the stairs at school, yet here he is, holding his friend. Maybe Zola was the only one allowed to touch him like this. Or perhaps it isn't true.

Jeffrey had read all about Cézanne's fear of touch in his mother's book. And in the DVD interview, the director, J-P McKeown, cited Annie Yeung as having helped him 'understand' the character of Cézanne, as if such a thing was possible, as if the different perspectives of a genius' life, or anyone's life, could be arranged and ordered to present a whole being.

He takes up his own copy of the book — slim, worn, the pale grey hardcover darkened with years of holding — from his bedside table. Between its pages, mother and son speak to each other, Annie's voice made from the whisper of flicked leaves.

She has already explained to Jeffrey that Cézanne's reaction to being bullied at school was extreme, but not one he was able to control, and showed him how Zola helped him through those difficult days.

She's told him about Cézanne's father, too, whose attempts to control his son with blackmail and outright hostility, the threats to cut off his allowance, tainted their relationship. *At least your father has not done that*, he has heard her say. *If it were not for him, you wouldn't be able to create, or share, your own art.*

As Lone Wolf, the most famous digital guerilla artist on the planet, he's able to send his work to every computer in the world, bypassing all firewall technology, spam filters, State censors and content blockers — he is the subject of news reports, TV documentaries, speculative magazine features, unofficial cyber-retrospectives, international conferences, academic dissertations, blog forums, monographs, journal articles

138

and, perhaps most flatteringly, forgery. None of this concerns Jeffrey at all. What matters to him is the dissemination of his work. After that, people can do what they like with it.

Yes, Walter provides him with everything he needs and it's only because his father allows him access to CantoCorp's systems and resources that he is able to do what he does and no one knows his location, or his identity. But he won't give his father credit for any of it. Wasn't it the least Walter could do? Jeffrey is his son after all, and a son is not a shiny trophy to show off to friends and associates that you put away when it becomes tarnished.

Your father didn't put you away, Annie whispers. *You did that to yourself.*

He has no reply to that.

Jeffrey's living quarters, in which he has stayed for the last ten years, are directly below the CantoCorp penthouse. Generously proportioned and self-contained with sound-proofing so effective Jeffrey may as well be in another building all together, he loves their restrained, chocolate and beige elegance because it reminds him of the Mandarin Oriental.

His father would never cut the power, or the water, or the air con, as he had initially threatened to do. For all the blustering about how little he cared for others' views of him, Jeffrey's instinct had been that Walter would not want to be seen as a bad father and that the minimum amount of fuss following his decision to become Hikikomori was best for everyone. He could easily lie about Jeffrey's whereabouts, or play on people's sympathy regarding his son's self-imposed isolation if he wanted, it didn't matter. As it was, Walter simply never mentioned him. Jeffrey was like a flower in that respect.

He is happy to reap the rewards of his father's guilt, and the past ten years have gone quick enough. His food is delivered whenever he asks for it, his clothes and towels and bed linen all laundered and returned within twenty-four hours. He keeps the place spotless himself. Any equipment he orders is left outside the door and all Jeffrey need do is lean across the threshold to take it in. He has his running machine, his free weights, his computers, books, music, wants for nothing in fact. He is not much interested in what his mother has to say about this.

The pause function on the movie times out and it starts up again. Zola and Cézanne pull apart and make their way down the street, arm in arm, Émile chatting, gesticulating warmly, Paul's face relaxing into a thoughtful smile. The moment of the two men embracing makes sense if what matters is showing how deep their friendship runs, which is the truth of that scene.

Jeffrey has explained to Annie that he and Cézanne were about the same age when each suffered the violence that was done to them; Cézanne kicked down the stairs and Gor Gor's death, which Jeffrey felt as physically as an assault, and his response to it was as much beyond his control as Cézanne's fear of being touched was. That's what he tells her.

At least Cézanne had Zola to protect him, but Jeffrey has no one. Gor Gor understood him more than anyone ever could. He and Leslie were as inseparable Zola and Cézanne had been.

But…

Yes, he knows no one is inseparable! Gor Gor and he were separated, weren't they? He and Walter Junior… they should have been inseparable too. And their mother also; she was taken from him and no one can tell him why. Why were they all separated?

This time, it's Annie who has no answer.

He has his friends. He receives so many messages, so many other invisible voices, he can reply to only a tiny proportion. Some post video tributes to him on YouTube, and there has even been fanfic written in which Lone Wolf appears as a character. He's developed ongoing communication and true friendship with a small number, privately. They feel they know him, some say, and that he knows them, or a part of them in him, which makes them feel they know themselves more in turn. They write to him the things they couldn't say to anyone else, though he does not reciprocate in that respect. He doesn't tell them he is a twenty-five-year-old man who hasn't left his room for a decade, who has conversations with his dead mother and loathes his soon-to-be-dead father. None can touch him as Zola hugs Cézanne, or Leslie and Marius joking around on the red carpet, or the doctor laying a soothing hand on his father's arm. He can't remember that last time he was touched.

One friend, the painter Sophie Greene, has been a particular favourite. Over the last couple of years they've developed a real bond and if he's come close to revealing his identity to anyone, it's her. During one of his digital conferences, she casually quoted a line from his mother's book which he instantly responded to, though carefully, paranoid about giving his identity away. He'd given her access then to his personal forum, letting her in to his inner circle and she'd shared how one of his digital interventions had come at a time when she was feeling extremely vulnerable.

She'd gotten back together with her on-off-on-again ex-husband — some useless poet guy, apparently — and then ended the relationship again — "and for *good* this time!" He may be the father of her child, she'd written Jeffrey, but she couldn't take his mood swings and erratic behaviour any more. One day, in the middle of it all, her phone had pinged and she'd opened the message expecting another desperate tirade from this Joel and, instead, there was Lone Wolf's latest work, a never-ending shower of blooms that had beamed around the world but which, she felt, had been sent to her only.

This meant a lot to Jeffrey because he'd only recently — this was 2011, he seems to recall — felt brave enough to start making flower pieces and, unusually, he'd not only replied directly to her thank you but asked questions about her and her relationship with her ex and then, after Googling her, he'd let her know how much he liked her work, her self-portraits especially, and was interested in its development.

He was aware of idealising Sophie, for a period, as a beautiful young mother, which in itself gave birth to strange, imagined memories in which she replaced his own, Sophie's and Annie's voice and face merging into one. He'd taken some time out to process, to compartmentalise, before entering back into their dialogue — they were not Inseparables, Jeffrey and she, but he recognised a friendship that was important, and precious.

Opening up his mother's book, he turns to the dedication page:

In memory of my adored wife An-Xie Yeung (1960 - 1990)
and Walter Yeung Junior (1988 - 1990),
and for Jeffrey Yeung, my only living hope, with love.

In the short preface Walter writes that he had wanted to publish his wife's book posthumously, as proof that she had once existed in the world and Jeffrey has often asked her, when reading this, "Aren't I that proof, mother?"

Currently, his favourite section is about a painting in New York's Metropolitan Museum, *Still Life with Apples and a Pot of Primroses*. Annie reads the apples nestled amongst folds of a tablecloth as suggesting domestic warmth and comfort. The cloth protects and nurtures them, like arms enfolding. At some point, he worked out that she was writing this book while undergoing her IVF treatment, and he imagines her filled with yearning as she writes.

A quick tap at his keyboard calls up the very painting. He fills his bank of screens with it, bathes in its bright blue and orange glow. It's like the sun coming out, like laughter. He is so lonely sometimes.

There are two small apples, one green, one red, sitting side by side at the front of the table. He thinks he can smell them, those apples. He and Walter Junior would have been exactly like that once, nestled inside their mother.

Right now, the focus of his own work is all on creating his most spectacular digital bouquet. '*Flowers for Gor Gor*' will be delivered to the whole world, a gift and a tribute on the occasion of the tenth anniversary of Leslie's tragic suicide.

He wants to remind people of their connection to the natural world, playing with its inbuilt paradox, given that the flowers aren't real, and a nostalgia for things he himself no longer experiences. He hasn't touched, smelled, or even *seen* a real flower since Leslie's 49th day. He still orders them occasionally, in the hope that they will slip through his father's perverse restriction and arrive outside his door, but they never do. Walter still asserts that power in their relationship. Perhaps, afterwards, there can be flowers once again.

It's the only thing he has ever refused you, Jeffrey. Surely you can you understand why?

Yes, yes, he understands. He knows full well the part flowers played in his own family tragedy and, as a result, '*Flowers for Gor Gor*' contains a very specific and unbearable sense of loss that he's only now able to express; a floral tribute not just to Leslie, but to the three most important people in his life, all of them dead. At least this bouquet will not rot on the sidewalk.

Jeffrey taps at the keyboard, wanting to see Walter, and finds him in his bedroom, sleeping. He spends most of his time asleep these days, or simply lying with his eyes closed, earphones in, listening to no doubt God-awful music. He'll leave him to it.

He clicks through the security cameras, flitting around the

headquarters of CantoCorp, which is calm and quiet, as if the images are all frozen, or still lifes. Walter has not been seen for weeks and rumours are circulating, building in intensity. He used to stalk the corridors every day, keeping everyone on their toes, controlling everything with his legendary charisma, so-called. Now, at the closing of the Walter Yeung era, there is only a subdued sense of crisis, dampened by a blind faith that CantoCorp is too big to fail and everything is in place for a smooth transition. Jeffrey has only sporadically considered what this might mean for him. What will he become?

One screen is crackling and fizzing with dynamic force, he sees — the room with the painting machine. Jeffrey sits up to watch, re-charged by its energy. This machine has always struck him as strangely antiquated. With its complex workings on view, the nuts and bolts and wheels and joints all rendered in glittering CantoCorp steel, it's like something from 1960s sci-fi, or a steampunk fantasy, the past's version of the future. Its many arms, fitted with different sized paintbrushes and palette knives — one even has a prosthetic hand for finger and thumb smudging! — dab, jab, spin and stroke.

What can it be doing at this hour, at this particular point in his father's life? Jeffrey would not put it past him, even so near death, to be planning some last ridiculous spectacle, a prank to be played at his art museum's opening, perhaps.

What a waste of money, technology and time simply to make fools of some art experts. What a failure of the imagination not to use all of this technology to create something truly stimulating. Walter's idea of the painting machine is pointless — yet another way of exercising his power, not just over those who work for him and those around him, but even over dead, great artists whose unique abilities and individuality he must hate.

The end product will be the result of hours of scanning and processing of an original work of art. All the necessary information — exact layering of paint, gradations of colour, angle of strokes, the varying thickness of the surface — will have been analysed and fed back into this machine in order to reproduce it as faithfully and accurately as possible. If it were up to Jeffrey, if he had his father's infinite resources, he would create something a million million times better than a ridiculous painting machine: virtual reality landscapes, copied from paintings, that you could actually *be* in, actually *feel*. Maybe he will, as a future project. '*Flowers for Gor Gor*' will be, he has already decided, his last floral work. It's time for a change of direction.

He visualises himself walking in the countryside at the foot of Mont Sainte-Victoire; the houses, the fields, the trees, constructed of planes of blue, green, orange and white, the sky a scribbling of blue paint, darker in some patches, the canvas showing through sometimes like a tear in the fabric of the universe. He's accompanied by his mother now, walking up the mountain together, right to the top, to survey the beauty of the world she loved, Cézanne's world, because his paintings spoke to her in ways his father would never fully understand, and, perhaps, neither would he, though he has read her book over and over.

He finds himself smiling, imagines reaching in to *Still Life with Apples and a Pot of Primroses*, the blossoms silky-pink against his fingertips, and takes an apple from the table — the bright red-orange-green one on the far left — the little pile of apples collapses around it. He smells apples again, takes a bite and it tastes sour-sweet and juicy, just as he thought it would be.

Emerging from this reverie, he taps his keyboard and the bank of screens fills with a single image of the painting machine at work. All but smothered by it, Jeffrey spots an easel with a canvas resting on it, and zooms in. Which of Walter's prized masterpieces is it to be this time?

He can't quite see past the flailing robotic arms, will have to wait for a pause in the action... then — *there*! — Jeffrey jumps up.

Walter bought this painting in secret, he knows, and his mother's love for these apples is expressed often enough in her book for Jeffrey to understand why he had bought it.

Jeffrey returns to his desk, switches to the camera in his father's suite. Sure enough, there, on the wall in front of Walter's favourite armchair, where *Still Life with Apples and Jug of Flowers* usually resides and has faced him throughout his whole illness, hangs instead the star of Walter's birthday prank, three months ago; 'Cézanne's *Landscape, Mont Sainte-Victoire*.

He wouldn't be seeking to reveal his ownership of it now, would he? Through another stupid game that he isn't even well enough to witness? No, something else must be happening. But what... What game is he playing?

Maria & Nick, Liverpool — 2008

"I was starting to think you weren't coming."

Maria waves her phone. "Sorry. Mad busy. Anyway, I'm not *that* late." She leans past him, pulls the drawing towards them. She'll dive right in but try and keep things light. "What's this then?"

"Oh, not much. It's been a while, you know. I was thinking about school. Paddy's classes, d'you remember?"

"Do I? God, the things Paddy used to make us draw. He must have retired years ago by now. He's probably still trawling Crosby Sands for bits of old bleached wood. They'll be all piled up somewhere with no one to look at them. He looked like a bit of old stick himself, d'you remember?" He stays quiet, is looking closely at his drawing, so she pulls a chair up and waits.

She's nervous, Nick thinks, gabbing away like that. She's doesn't know how to say what she's got to say. He clocks that she's gripping her phone really tight and her eyes are still assessing the drawing, darting over it, looking for a diagnosis on the paper that tells her exactly how he's doing. It's obvious she's seeing someone else.

It's nearly a year since she moved out. He'd spent the first six months in shock, numb as anything, and then it finally hit, one morning when he couldn't lift his head off the pillow and he thought he must be getting flu or something, then realised what was coming and called Doctor Hartmann.

At these times, there's a mountain of feelings inside him, so many there's no way to express them, because where would he start? Hartmann asked him once, "How do you climb a mountain, Nick?" and Nick had sat in silence, a silence Hartmann refused to fill for him, for what felt like ages, until eventually he'd managed to whisper, "One step at a time, until you get to the top." Doctor Hartmann had nodded to him, pleased, and Nick always tried to please him in the way that he'd tried to please Paddy, and this was because he never could please Jimmy.

He'll ask her straight out: *Maria, are you seeing somebody?* But those words are not words that he's practised, and he feels them solidify in his chest at the thought, and his mouth needs liquid words if he's to be able to speak them. How did they get this far deep into each other's lives without being able to speak properly to each other?

He'll close his eyes and rest his head on the table, go to sleep until it all disappears, this awful uncertainty. Maria's face that he's seen and known in love, in fear, in joy, in pain, can still be new and strange and frightening to him. And that's how it happens, he thinks, that no matter how deep you are in another person's life, there are still new things to say that can't easily be said because of how frightening the next thing said would be, and then the next thing, and the thing after that.

Maria wonders what she can say about the drawing that'll open up the path to the other things she needs to say? There's a good knife in the foreground, probably as good as anything she's ever seen him do. He's got the distinction between the wooden handle and the metal blade's surface spot on and the foreshortening's really good too. She'll tell all that to him in a moment.

She was always able to see like this, but was embarrassed to say so out loud, and sometimes when she did Nick made it worse. He could be cruel, like Jimmy, not violent but belittling, especially when it came to her commenting on his work. The apple half has a pip sort of hanging out from the middle and she feels this urge to reach in to the drawing and save it before it falls, because this is what she does — she tries to save things — but she must focus that urge on herself now.

Maria wants to say, I've had an amazing week, Nick. One of the best of my life, actually.

She wants to say, You're the person I'd most like to share this with, even though it's a secret, you're the one who'd most understand what J-P's offer means to me. It'll really mean the end of them, she knows, but she has to do it.

She wants to tell him that, when she'd been sent by the Film Office to meet J-P and Marius at the airport, she and J-P had taken an instant shine to each other. This was a homecoming for him, and he'd asked her lots of questions about the changes to the city and all that, and during the taxi ride to the hotel she'd turned round at one point and spied the pair of them holding hands and Marius had pulled away, pointing out the window, asking, "What's that?" and "What's that?" and she'd answered him like they were already friends, even though they'd only just met, wasn't intimidated by them at all.

And she wants to tell him about J-P taking her out for dinner and saying how much he enjoyed working with her, how he really liked having her around. They'd talked about growing up in Liverpool, and realised they'd gone to the same cafés and clothes shops, even been at certain clubs on the same night, at certain gigs, they discovered, and she'd not hesitated for a second when he asked her if she'd come to L.A.

and work as their personal assistant because he and Marius needed someone they both liked and could trust.

And she wants to say it's all like a dream, that she'll miss him but she has to go and it's for the best because they both have to move on with their lives, though she knows this means something different for him than it does for her.

She wants to say that she loves him but, she's sorry, she's not *in* love with him anymore and they both deserve to be loved and in love, and this is for the best and doesn't he think so?

She can't bear to hurt him. He's had so much hurt and fear in his life and she hates the thought of adding to it. Maybe this is how Jimmy felt just before laying into him — hating himself for hurting Nick but not being able to stop. And that thought makes her go cold because she knows she's *not* like Jimmy who had no bloody excuse, but still she can't bear the thought of the pain she's about to cause. It's impossible.

She thinks again of Jimmy burning in the car and what pain he must have been in to do what he did. No one ever knew what was going on in Jimmy's head, but being burned alive was less painful than the pain he could see no end of, and it must have been torture to be trapped between those two things. She tries to imagine ever feeling like that, and can't. She wants to apologise for all of it, even though none of it is her fault.

I'm going away to work in America with J-P, she wants to tell him, and I'm saying goodbye to you today, now, because I don't think it would be a good idea for us to see each other again before I go, which is in three weeks' time when my visa's been sorted, and I wish I could make your pain go away but I can't, because I've tried all my life and it hasn't worked, and it's not my fault and I have to stop now because I'm tired and I don't love you anymore and I'm sorry, but it's not my fault.

She's terrified because she's about to do the second worst thing that any one has ever done to him, maybe the worst thing, worse than finding his dad on fire. And she's suddenly so angry with him she could smack him across the face to make him understand how hard he's making this for her and it's not her fault. How can she say it? She *has* to say it.

And what she says, pushing the drawing away, is, "So, how've you been?"

What should he come out with? I'm falling apart thanks, how're you? Or, I'm a bit spooked out to be honest because that Cézanne painting you told me to come and see is really disturbing and I think I can hear that woman's thoughts, the woman being murdered. Her voice floats down from the atrium again: *Help me, Oh, please save me, Dear God, let it be over.*

He doesn't want her to worry about him drawing, which he knows she is. He'd rather she's worried he knows what she's up to. It's her not telling him that makes him anxious. It's that what's making him think a painting of a murder is speaking to him, words coming from the mouth of the woman being killed, from the terrible sky, from the knife raised in the killer's hand, words he can't face.

He takes hold of the fruit knife and rolls it around in his hand. He sees himself pressing the fruit knife's blade against the ticklish flesh of his inner arm, cutting himself to make the words stop, to make Maria see, but he doesn't. He says, "I'm not too bad, thanks."

She nods. "Have you eaten already?"

"No, I just had a snack. The other half of that apple. I was hungry but I'm not now. Are you hungry?"

"No. There's food all day on the set. I had *two* breakfasts." She laughs and rubs her stomach but he doesn't react, so she says, "Nick, I'm sorry I was a bit late. It's been frantic today like you wouldn't believe. They had all these girls getting autographs from Marius. One of them turned up in her pyjamas — can you believe it! — and we told her she couldn't have her photo taken with him looking like that and then she kicked off and we had to have her escorted away by security."

She puts her phone down on the table and reaches over and takes his cup of tea from the tray and slurps it down and holds the empty cup in her two hands and thinks, she's ruined it now because she moved the cup.

"It's good," she says, "your drawing. The apple's great, and the knife's amazing. Dead life-like."

"It's not bad," he says. "I was just waiting and thought I'd give it a go. It's been a while." He picks up a pencil and starts in on the drawing again. He's bent right over it so she can't see what he's doing. After a moment, he says, "You don't need to worry, you know," but he doesn't look at her. He keeps on at the drawing.

"Okay. That's good. I won't worry then." She might as well take a running jump at it. "But Nick, there's something I need to talk to you about."

He puts his pencil down but still doesn't look at her. "I know."

"You know? Nick, look at me, will you." God, he makes her angry sometimes. "What do you *know*?"

"About him."

She frowns. He knows about J-P's offer? That she's leaving? How can he know?

"Your new boyfriend," Nick says, "*lover*, whatever he is."

"My — ?" she can't help but laugh — "I haven't got a — a new boyfriend, Nick. Bloody chance'd be a fine thing."

"Don't fucking take the piss with me Maria," he says, facing up to her now.

"Nick, look, I haven't got anyone." She puts her hands on his trembling hands. "You're imagining things." It's dangerous to say this to him.

He pushes her away, pushes the drawing away. It slides off the table and falls to the floor.

"I can't be doing with this, Nick. It's work, you know it is. Marius and J-P — "

"Oh, Marius and J-P, Marius and J-P. That's all you can talk about these days. What the fuck kind of name is J-P anyway? Pretentious wanker."

Maria sighs. "God, will you listen to yourself?" His snarling at her only makes her stronger in the face of it. "Look, there's something important I need to talk to you about, seriously. It's about us."

"Us?" He gulps the word out. Does she want to get back with him?

"Nick, I know you've had a tough year, it's not been easy for either of us but something's happened and I need to tell you about it. I've been offered a job. J-P's offered me a job. As his personal assistant. It means moving to America. And I want to go. I'm going." He looks totally dazed, but she can't stop now. She already feels better. "I thought working at the Film Office was a dream come true but this, this is unreal, the best chance I'll ever have. I've given in my notice this morning. They owe me some holiday so I'm leaving in three weeks — "

"Three — ?"

"I'm sorry Nick. I'm really sorry."

"Three weeks? You're leaving?"

Maria nods.

Nick shakes his head at her. "I don't want you to."

"Nick, listen, I've decided."

"You won't change your — "

"No, Nick. It's settled."

"There's nothing — " He wants to put up more of a fight but he hasn't the energy to even finish his sentence.

Maria's mobile lights up and vibrates across the table top, rattling the tea things. She reaches for her phone but Nick grabs at it, getting there first, and shouts "Fuck *off*." into it before tossing it back down on the table.

"Oh Nick, for Christ's sake — "

"That was him," he spits at her. "So he wants you to go to America with him does he? Will you live with him? Are you two fucking?"

This is one of those times when he reminds her of Jimmy and she doesn't know what to do, what to say, because she's frightened of him. But she's not going to be Sue, she's not going to be his mum. She doesn't owe him anything.

"How many times do I have to — ? No, I'm not Nick. It's *work*."

"I don't believe you. Why can't you tell me? Just be honest."

But she can't tell him that of course she's not sleeping with J-P because J-P is sleeping with Marius. She can't say those words aloud because she'd risk losing everything if their secret came out and she doesn't trust Nick not to tell people, or phone the papers, just to spite her, to ruin it all.

It takes all her effort to say, "I *am* being honest with you. Look, Nick — " and she stoops to pick up the drawing and sees the knife blade drawn there, so real that her fear simply vanishes, and she imagines herself as the steel blade of that knife in the drawing — cold and sharp and purposeful — "I need to leave you." And she imagines then that she's Jimmy, getting out of the car and going to the boot and taking the can of petrol and getting back in the car and unscrewing the lid and pouring it over himself and it's awful but it took some real strength, what he did.

"Please, Maria," Nick says, his face desperate. "I can't do it on my own. You have to stay and help me."

"I *can't*, Nick. I can't." She takes his hands in hers again, but he turns away. "Listen, you don't have to be on your own. There's plenty of people who'll help you but I can't do it. I've tried, haven't I? Maybe that's the problem. I'm holding you back there, where you shouldn't be. Every time you look at me you see all the terrible things that've ever happened to you, because I was there for every one of them, wasn't I? If I leave then you can really start again." She doesn't think she believes this, but wishes it could be true.

"But you *weren't* there when Jimmy was in the car."

"I know, Nick, and God help me but I'm glad I wasn't because imagining it is bad enough. Every time I see a fire — "

And Nick is looking at her like an excited boy, and says, "No, I mean before."

"Before? What do you mean, before?"

This'll change her mind, this telling her his big secret. Those other solid words have now begun to liquefy, are about to erupt. It'll change the whole landscape. "I got to the car park before the fire."

"Jesus, Nick. What are you saying this for?"

"Because it's the truth, right! I saw Jimmy coming out the pub and I watched him stagger to the car and I thought, he's not going to drive is he? He'll kill himself. And I thought it would be okay if he died, that I'd like that, but then I thought that he might hurt someone else if he crashed and if he tries to drive away I'll have to stop him. But he was just sat in the car, until I thought he'd gone to sleep, and I was shitting myself then because, if he was asleep, I'd have to knock on the window and wake him up and he'd batter me for it, but my mum had sent me to get him, so I had to. And I was just about to go over when he opened the car door and got out and went to the boot and took the can of petrol out and, d'you know what?" — Nick laughs, breathlessly — "I thought he was going to drink it. I thought he'd run out of money and was so desperate to get off his face that he was going to drink the petrol, and then we'd *really* be in for it when he got home. And I watched him get back in the driver's seat, take the lid off the can and lift it up, and I thought, you *dirty bastard*, drinking fucking petrol. But he never. He held it over his head and poured it all over him until there was none left. And I knew. I knew what he was going to do, and I could have stopped him but I didn't. I thought, Go on then you, do it if you're going to do it. And I would have done it for him if he'd asked me because I hated him right then more than I'd ever hated him when he was beating me up, or beating my mum up, because he was a selfish fucking *bastard* to be doing that. But then I thought — she loves him, the stupid cow. She loves him more than she loves me because if she loved me more she'd have left him and taken me with her and wouldn't let him do what he did to me. And I didn't know what to do because I knew she'd be devastated, but why did she never stop him Maria?"

"I don't know, Nick," is all Maria can say. "It wasn't her fault, but I don't know why."

"So I walked towards the car and stood there and I could see the door wasn't locked and I could've opened the door and let the air out and stopped him taking the matches out. And it took him four goes Maria, *four* goes! Because his hands were shaking that much the matches kept breaking, and it was ages, and I didn't do anything. I didn't do anything. And then, when the fourth match lit, it was like a —— an *explosion* —— and I jumped back, but nothing happened to me, and I swear there was a bit when he was all on fire and had his hands on the steering wheel and that was all on fire too, when he turned to me and he looked like the fucking devil, and then I couldn't see anything else because the windows had gone all black, and Jimmy was all burning, and that's when I ran to the pub and hammered on the door. And I've ne — ne — " his sobbing words echo around the café all the way up

156

to the atrium above, and Maria can sense people looking at them, but she keeps tight hold of Nick's hands and focuses on his face because that's the most important thing right now — "never to-told, anyone before — not my mum, not Hartmann, and not even you, because I kno-know it was wrong and I should ha-have stopped him but I was frightened he-he'd take it out on me. Because I'd seen him pour the petrol on himself and then stopped him, like that was the worst thing I could do to him, have se-seen him like that, and I knew, I knew that he'd never let me off for saving him, and that every time he-he'd beat me up he'd see me *there* in the car park and that would just make it worse, make him hit me harder. So I let him bu-burn himself to death because I was scared of him living."

Nick buries his face in the backs of her hands that are holding his, and wipes his tears away with her hands and Maria rests her cheek on the crown of his head.

"Shhh, Nick. It's okay... Shhhhhh..."

And he says, his face still buried in the back of her hands, "I'm just like him, d'you know that? I'm just like my dad."

"No you're not, Nick, you're nothing like him."

"I am. I'm a selfish fucking *cunt* who takes it out on other people. People they love."

"No, shhh..."

"I never hit you though, did I, but I'm just as bad. Trapping you like Jimmy trapped me and mum. That's why you moved out. And you were right to."

Her phone rings again. She needs to get back, to get away from this. "Nick, I'm sorry, but I really need to go."

He looks up, his confused face all wet and red. It's not worked. "Go where?"

157

She nearly says America, but instead she says, "I've got to be back at work. The schedule's really tight and there isn't the money. They need me."

"They need you? *I* need you."

"Yes, I know you do, but — " Her phone is still ringing.

And then it's all so clear to him. "I ju- I just need to let the air out."

"What?"

"The air. In the car. I mean — the picture."

"What picture?"

"I couldn't save him. But I can save her."

"Who Nick? I don't understand — "

"In the picture."

"Nick, love, please, I've got no *time* for this. I've really got to go."

He stands up, takes a big gulp of breath. "Come up with me. It won't take long. Come with me, Maria."

"Nick — "

"Please?"

She looks at his face and this is the hardest thing she's ever had to do, though it feels easy as soon she's done it, which is to say, "No."

He flushes redder and shouts at her, "Fuck you then!" Pushes past her towards the main stairs.

She not going to follow him. She's not, but he sees him reach into his pocket and pull out something, the fruit knife, the one from his drawing. What's he going to do?

She shouts after him, runs past all the people looking at them and up the stone steps, sees him disappear into one of the rooms, and follows.

Joel, New York — 2010

Central Park in spring and everything looked new. The day's pale light picked out the buds and branches, sketching them on the grass, on the wooden benches, on the spongy tarmac of the Mall underfoot. Kids running round in expanding arcs, the trundling of serious-faced skateboarders, a dog walker's forearms tensed against a bunch of straining leashes, and a jogger approaching, waving away a fly in front of her face. All new.

Joel could smell the newness, like freshly laundered sheets and hard, striped candy. Somewhere across the park a guy was playing the sax; a distant music, not really music but a free-form honk and squeal, irritating and difficult to ignore. He counted down the line of trees as he walked to push the squawking out of his head, right up until he stopped and sat on the bench, when the saxophone burrowed into him again.

He stretched an arm out along the wooden backrest and traced with his finger the outline of the daisy carved into it. The benches had these flowers all along them, and Joel loved their simplicity, like a child's drawing. He loved how they were smoothed and warmed by years of human contact and thought of all the people from the past who'd stroked them, as he did. He felt totally secure on the curve of this bench in front of the bandstand's small plaza. It was his favourite spot in the whole park and that's why he'd chosen it for today.

Around the plaza, a dreadlocked in-line skater was executing wide, graceful loops. His bright orange bodysuit and matching helmet, his muscular certainty, sparked an image, of Apollo, driving his chariot across the sky. He took out his notebook. He wrote, *Apollo Skates in Central Park*. A title? Or a first line, maybe? Joel wrote down the word '*resplendent*', — the only word for this guy — and, then... then, nothing. His ability to think of anything beyond a fragmented image had left him a while back, maybe for good. He still carried his notebook and pencil everywhere, though these days they acted only as hostile witnesses to his great doubt, gave testimony to his inability to produce anything worthwhile.

Why had he suggested that he and Sophie go see this bullshit movie together? Because it was about her favourite painter that's why, and he wanted her to know that he still knew that. Then she'd said, "Let's go to the Museum first, to the Cézanne rooms," because the Met were doing a cut-price-ticket/movie-tie-in.

Oh, and it was starring, of all people, Marius Woolf — "Isn't that an *amazing* coincidence? — the actor who'd bought her first show, who'd bank-rolled them for basically two whole years as well as paying for their modest, secret wedding.

He heard that saxophone again and, somewhere, a kid crying. A firm sting pricked the back of his hand and he looked down to see, not some angry insect, but that he was jabbing the point of the pencil into it. He stopped himself, licked the welt he'd made, to soothe it.

A woman came and sat on the bench further along. She was pulling an empty buggy with one hand and gripping a little boy's arm with the other, pleading softly with him. "C'mon sweetie, you're just *tired*. Drink your juice, c'mon."

160

The kid squirmed and pulled away to stand a few paces back from her. She glanced up at Joel who gave her a sympathetic smile, and she rolled her eyes in response. The boy turned to look at him, licking snot and tears from his top lip, then tottered towards him, looking back at his mom the whole time, as if testing the limits she'd set to the approaching of strangers.

"Hey buddy," Joel said. He'd help this kid and his mom, try to close the gap between the two of them. From his notebook he tore the page with his scratched, useless words on it, placed the paper on top of the carved wooden daisy, and began to rub his pencil over it.

The boy drew nearer as he worked, watching the flower emerge like a magic trick. When Joel finished he held it out to him, but he turned to his mom — there was the kid's limit, Joel thought. He's a good kid. When his mom nodded, he came forward to take it.

"It's a flower," Joel said. "See?" The boy grasped the wondrous piece of paper unsmiling. "It's for your mom," Joel said. "Go give your mom the flower."

In a burst of confident relief, he trotted across to her, holding the paper up and out. "Oh *thank* you honey," she said, taking it from him. "Did you say thank you?"

The boy shook his head, clambered into the buggy and shoved the juice cup into his mouth.

"I'm so sorry," the woman said, stroking her son's sleepy head. "He's crabby today. He's usually very polite."

"No problem," Joel said. "I have one of my own. About the same age. A girl."

"Ah, I thought you might be a dad."

Joel didn't want to talk to this nice woman about being a dad, didn't want to answer questions about his daughter, his divorce, custody arrangements, shared parenting. He didn't want her to know his marriage to Sophie had fallen apart right after Imogen was born. He wanted her to think he was a great father and a husband who took good care of his family, not some dick who'd thrown away his only chance at happiness.

From his buggy the boy studied him, struggling now to keep his eyes open. Joel fought the same sensation, as if the kid's tired stress was infectious. Christ, he was exhausted. He wanted to shut everything out and go to sleep, but he mustn't do that. He had to be alert for when Sophie arrived.

Four years down the line he was still putting himself through this shit. He should have just jacked off in the shower this morning and gotten her out of his system, rinsing her down the plughole with his load. He screwed his eyes shut and shook his head at the ugly thought. It had been his idea, hadn't it, to go to the movies?

He screwed up the notebook in his lap and threw it at the trashcan by the bench. It missed the target and dropped to the floor. "Best place for it," he said.

The woman got up and, tucking things away in the bottom of the buggy, walked off down the Mall. Joel tried to catch her eye to give her a goodbye smile, but she was avoiding his gaze, he was sure. He was a muttering freak, throwing his stuff at the trash like that. He wouldn't want to sit near him neither, especially not with a kid. He gripped the pencil, his knuckles hard as bullets, to stop himself from calling out after her.

Instead, he directed his attention back to Apollo, whirling around the plaza, faster now and backwards, one leg crossing behind the other, a couple of dreadlocks stuck to his sweat-sheened cheek. The efficient regularity of his smooth glide was beautifully calming and Joel relaxed the hand that was tingling, visualised the blood flowing back into his fingers.

The pencil's gold lettering had worn down to almost nothing, its red covering chipped and totally gone in places. He bit down on it, breaking off a slither of wood that he rolled around in his mouth. It tasted of something over and done with, something dead. It was not like the wood of the bench, which still had something to offer, some support.

He'd brought with him her copy of Annie Yeung's *Shadow is a Colour as Light is*, which she thought was lost, but which he had taken, hidden, and kept as a talisman of sorts. More than a reminder of Sophie it was a part of her. He'd known how much she'd be upset at losing it, and he wanted her to feel that loss. But today, he was going to give it back to her.

He'd said to her, "I'll be on the curve of the bench, opposite the bandstand, just like old times," that last bit a joke, but he hadn't thought how it might make her feel to meet him there, or how it would make him feel either. "Revisiting old friends," he'd said, meaning the paintings, but she could've assumed he thought of her only as a friend now and that was the direction they'd take from this moment on, as decided by him.

Three years ago, almost to the day, Joel and Sophie had married after being together just ten months, and they'd done it without telling anyone.

According to his father, whose language when it came to Joel turned old-school and florid, it was 'an act of indescribable folly in this day and age' to marry someone so soon after meeting, 'unless you have to', as if it had been ten days not ten months, as if anyone had to get married in this day and age. It was also 'preposterous and harebrained' of them to start a family the year after that, when they were both only twenty-five, struggling to make ends meet and neither of them established in their careers ('if you can *have* such a thing as a career in poetry'). But Joel didn't care, and neither did Sophie.

At every stage they'd told themselves, each other, their friends, her

163

parents, his father, that they knew exactly what they were getting into. If Joel's dad had known exactly what they were planning he would have coerced him into calling the whole thing off, but Joel had been willing to defy him and face the consequences, strong enough to do that for the first time in his life.

He managed to convince Sophie that what they were doing was romantic, exciting even. "Imagine what a story we'll have to tell our grandkids," he'd said.

Sophie had waved the kitchen knife at him, with which she was chopping scallions. "Joel, there won't *be* any grandkids if your dad cuts your balls off."

As far as she knew at this point, Joel's father was stern and somewhat scary. This was before she'd been introduced to him. She didn't yet know the extent to which he terrified Joel, or that what she had done by loving Joel and making him feel loved, was give him the power to say no to him, and the faith to believe that, whatever revenge he took, as long as he had Sophie he could survive it.

In the end his father capitulated, or so Joel had thought, but, in reality, he was merely biding his time before the moment when it all collapsed and he could gloat over the ruins. And it was only a matter of time before he and Sophie would realise their grand, stupid mistake in thinking love was enough to see them through, that the landscape of their marriage could survive the catastrophe of being planted in toxic soil, irrigated by poisoned water.

Then, after they split, it was, according to his dad, 'imbecilic' of them to divorce so quickly after their separation. Joel could hear him now, his performed anger barely masking his genuine, cynical amusement: "Christ sakes Poop, marriage isn't something you just try out!"

Poop was what his father had called Joel since he was little. He'd told Sophie that it was short for Nincompoop, when she'd blinked in surprise on hearing it, but this was another one of his lies. Truth was, the nickname stemmed from a particular incident that took place when Joel was seven years old.

He'd made a noise when coming down the stairs — not a loud noise, or an annoying noise, just a noise that, for his father at that particular time and when he was in a certain mood, was 'totally unacceptable'. Joel was instructed to sit in absolute silence, on a hard wooden chair in his father's study, in order to 'learn some self-control'.

After one whole hour, Joel had grown so stiff, his ass so sore, that he'd started to cry, but crying was noise, so the punishment must begin all over again. Having had no breakfast, he'd gotten so hungry he thought he was going to pass out. The only thing that kept him conscious was the discomfort he started to experience once he needed to use the bathroom. He didn't dare ask to be excused because speaking, he knew, was also noise. Eventually, inevitably, he'd pissed himself all over the rug in his father's study and then shit his pants in terror. But, rather than re-start the clock, as Joel anticipated, there'd been a different torture in store.

Joel was due at a school friend's birthday lunch. At the appointed time his father dragged Joel to the party in his soiled clothes, forcing him onto the subway, too, for added humiliation. Joel reeked of shit the whole time, and desperately hoped no one could fathom where the stench came from. But they could — he saw by the looks of disgust on their faces.

At the lunch party, his father had behaved normally, chit-chatting with the other parents as if there was nothing amiss, purposefully ignoring the same screwed-up nose and wrinkled brow expressions they'd witnessed on the subway, while Joel played with the other kids, himself pretending nothing was up in an effort to placate his dad, who might take him home immediately if he played along, showed he'd learned his lesson.

The total disgust the moment his stink reached the other party guests, all classmates of his, was the worst torture of all and, eventually, one of the kids had finally lost it with him, shouting "Get lost, *Poop!*" as Joel approached. His father thought this was 'priceless, just priceless!' and so took to using it himself.

A year into their marriage, Sophie became pregnant and Joel's growing anticipation of the baby's arrival unlocked sensations he'd thought were suppressed completely. He couldn't trust himself, or the shaming rage that spilled out into his notebooks, pouring beyond the confines of the ruled margin, the soft cover.

He developed a paranoid, insomniac fear of the kind of father he would turn out to be, despite himself. Lying awake in the night, he would visualise losing control and his heart would palpate with anxiety. There'd be something one day — a last straw, a tether's end — and he'd imagine, like a fragment of film playing over and over in his mind's eye, an arm lashing out, smashing, slamming, the child skidding, sprawling across the floor, full of tears, screaming, the soundtrack to his own silent rage. He was a monster in the making and began to wish the baby away before it was born.

But when Imogen arrived, he very quickly fell totally in love with her, quicker even than he'd fallen in love with Sophie, which could only mean she had to be protected from him. He did this by shunning her, completely and utterly. Implacable he was in the face of his beautiful wife's crying recriminations, and after barely two years of marriage, when Imogen was just eleven months old, Sophie had finally accepted what a low-life piece of shit he was, and left.

Joel was jabbing at his inner arm now, with his pencil again. this had been happening more and more often the past few months. He needed to move, so pulled himself up from the bench and went over to where his notebook lay splayed on the ground, picked it up and wiped the grime off it, onto his jeans.

The sick-sweet stench of rotting fruit from the trashcan cut through the light, the noise, his smarting arm, its tang smothering Joel. He heard his father voice, ordering him to eat the mouldy fruit he had taken from the kitchen garbage and presented him with as evidence of his son's 'sheer, disgusting, wastefulness', which would 'not be tolerated'.

He thought he might chuck up and took some deep breaths, moved away from the trash.

The skating Apollo skid-halted in front of him and began to execute a slow, tight spin, then speeding up, speeding up, a whirling orange sun, the light from him blinding Joel all of a sudden, who dropped to the ground hot then cold then hot again.

Apollo's reviving voice came through, low and easy. "Hey man, whassup down there? You okay?"

"Just a bit — fuzzy — s'all," Joel managed to say.

"Yeah, I have days like that too. Let me help you there."

Apollo held out both hands and Joel took them. Even on wheels he was strong enough to support Joel back onto his feet and help him to the bench.

"Can I get you somethin'? Some water maybe?"

Joel shook his head. "D'you know what? I'm fine. Thanks."

"Okay then. Take it easy my man." With that, Apollo swivelled away to resume his flight.

Joel slotted his notebook back in his pocket, and the pencil too that had rolled underneath the bench when he collapsed. He rubbed his hands, red and smarting from his fall, and the residue of Apollo's sure, dry touch.

Walter & Jeffrey, Hong Kong — 2013

Walter lies in bed, quite, quite still. He breathes deeply, calmly. The music had almost sent him to sleep but he thinks it was the camera's warning bleep that disturbed his meditation. Or perhaps merely that sense one has of being looked at, the one that turns your head in a crowded room. Either way, Jeffrey must be watching him.

Walter was aware of his son's surveillance capabilities even before he'd put them into action. Chief Security Officer, Gordon Li, had informed him of Jeffrey's plan to hack into CantoCorp's network of cameras the instant the transfer of money he had been offered landed in his bank account. It was the proof Li needed of the bribe his employer's son had proposed to him in return for his cooperation.

Walter insisted Li keep the money he had wanted to return and tripled his already generous salary as reward for his loyalty. Li would continue in his Security Chief role, having won Jeffrey's trust, and it was he who persuaded Walter to let Jeffrey press ahead with his plan, when Walter's initial, outraged reaction had been to cease his son's access to all computing facilities immediately and indefinitely.

"With respect, Mister Yeung," Li had advised him, "should you do that I fear you may lose your son permanently, and forever." Li had actually placed a hand on Walter's arm to stop him lifting the phone into which he would have given the order. No one else would have dared, but, given how it has all turned out, it proved to be a priceless intervention.

Walter's anger had subsided, replaced with a grudging admiration for his son's audacity and technical know-how. He was also mollified by the thought of Jeffrey wanting to see him and even hoped that, eventually, the cameras might bring them back together. He was wrong about that, but having lost one son already, as long as Jeffrey remained with him, he had a link to Walter Junior and Annie, as well as some fragment of hope for the future. So he'd allowed Li to carry on working with Jeffrey and Li even came up with the idea of the warning bleep on the cameras, to alert him when he was being watched. As the camera system had no sound, Jeffrey would never know and, over time, Walter came to imagine that Jeffrey was surveying him always. That way, he could perform every action he made for his son, a sort of controlled improvisation, or augmented reality.

But now, lying here, the time for play-acting is past; he has no energy for it, but contents himself with the simple thought that Jeffrey is there, on the other side of the lens, sharing his room in silent communion.

Three years after the whole arrangement began, Officer Li had come to Walter with some new information regarding Jeffrey's online activities. He showed him the digital artworks his son had begun to send out around the globe, told him Jeffrey was so highly skilled at hacking there wasn't a computer system anywhere on the planet he couldn't penetrate. He was causing quite a stir, apparently, while managing to keep his identity a total secret.

Initially, Walter struggled to understand why on earth his son didn't want people to know it was his digital still lifes and virtual bouquets they were receiving. What was the point otherwise? What if someone else claimed the glory? "He's tossing aside the chance to really make something of himself in the eyes of the world," he'd complained to Li, "just as when he shut himself away. He and I are not at all alike in this. It must be his mother in him."

It was then Li told Walter that Jeffrey had given himself the moniker *Lone Wolf*, "an apparent reference," he said, opening his notebook, "to the French painter Paul Cézanne."

Walter had shot him a look.

"Master Yeung has been gathering information on said painter, research which has been fairly extensive over a period of some months." Li showed Walter the spreadsheet, documenting his monitoring of Jeffrey's online activity.

"Also," Li continued gently, "he recently ordered a copy of your — your late wife's book on the subject. He has been studying it closely, I believe, given how often he searches its terms."

Li was nothing if not thorough, and his loyalty to him has been second only to the doctor's. Friends they could never have been, but inseparable they had become, by default.

It was all to do with Annie, of course it was. But it was he, Walter, who knew Annie, not Jeffrey. It was Walter who thought about her every day, and it was Walter who knew what Annie would have wanted him to do. Walter's strategy had to be one of long-term investment.

He instructed Li to do whatever it took to facilitate the dissemination of Jeffrey's artwork and protect his anonymity. "But he must never know — *never*, Li — that I am assisting him. It would ruin everything."

These past few weeks, since his confinement, his dear wife has been in his mind even more it seems, every waking and sleeping moment. So much love Walter has felt, and so much guilt and confusion. He has interrogated his memories of her and of their marriage to the point he no longer knows what he remembers, what he knows.

171

He has been confronted by the notion that, had she lived, Annie would not have liked the person he has become. But he also likes to think that, had she lived, he would not have become that person.

So it was her fault, was it? She wasn't a real woman at all, but your image of a woman, a nullifying force for good, smothering your own drive for power and domination — is that it?

He lets out a low, rattling sigh. Why can he not have one clear thought without those apples challenging him, torturing him? How much longer will it go on?

His hours of contemplation in their presence have revealed more about himself than he thought possible, and it has not been pleasant. Collecting art was a way of trying to get closer to Annie, placing her in his mind and in his heart, trying to imagine her liking him for it. But, in the end, instead of bringing them closer, it pushed them apart. His lack of real feeling for any of the paintings has only highlighted the gap between them. He used to be so certain of everything but, even if she'd survived the crash, would their marriage have survived?

You failed her. You treated Annie's love of art with a secret contempt.

Such pain. He could curl up tight, tight as an apple.

It is only as he approaches his end — *because* he approaches his end — that he has opened up to what a painting might be able to show him, something he'd previously dismissed as pointless.

The idea for the painting machine was to prove to himself, and everyone else, that what these artists did was nothing special, nothing he need try to understand. He was wrong about that, as he has been wrong about so much else.

Walter had hoped that Jeffrey's awareness of his illness, his watching him shrink and shrivel, would be enough to persuade him out of his rooms. If this was a movie, there'd be a touching bedside reconciliation.

That film he'd gladly fund. But his deep sadness at his own unutterable stupidity has only grown these last few months, along with the depth of Jeffrey's silence.

The only glimmer, for Walter, was being able to witness, along with everyone else, Lone Wolf's tribute to Leslie Cheung. '*Flowers for Gor Gor*', so seemingly real he thought he could smell them, had delighted and disturbed Walter. Their scent had drifted across his bed, called up and mixed with the memory of the flowers he'd plunged into when frantically searching for his baby son on that awful day. '*Flowers or Gor Gor*' was utterly beautiful, even he could see that, and it broke his heart.

He is able to pass a hand over his music player, still has the strength, just about. The voice of Leslie Cheung drifts across his consciousness... '*In my days of emptiness, questioning the meaning of life, you were there...*' this listening to his music a way of being close to Jeffrey, whose vaguely remembered voice and Leslie's recorded voice merge...

Jeffrey's life of self-imposed isolation is the same as the life Walter chose for himself after Annie and Walter Junior died. Walter had wanted Jeffrey around because he looked like his mother, but it also pained Walter to see Annie there, in Jeffrey. The child became a living *memento mori*; the face and form of Walter's dead beloved and the sole repository of all his hopes.

That first time he'd seen Annie, over thirty years ago, drifts across now... '*With courage we faced the challenge of life...*' Her slender figure leaning against the wall in the art gallery, the intriguing sense of meeting one's match... perhaps a myth, his delusion of instant compatibility.

He'd resented Jeffrey for living, a perverse reaction that he should have arrested the moment it arose. But that would have required a level of self-doubt, a level of awareness he did not possess back then. Now, he's not sure whether Jeffrey reminded him how much he had loved Annie, or whether he reminded him of his doubting that love. His son was a living admonishment, a second *memento mori* and this one for his marriage. Walter had put the child Jeffrey in his own room and only went there when he could face him, which was not often. Then, ten whole years ago, Jeffrey had put himself in there and never come out, just how Walter had shown him. '*If there's a chance for me to live again, I hope to meet you in the journey of life…*'

How wrong to think he could control everything. By overcoming their struggles to start a family, he had learned nothing tangible from those difficult early years…

'*Thank you for sticking by me in the stormiest days, and keeping me company in this journey of life.*'

Giving in to her desire to drive her and his sons herself… he has tried and tried and tried not to blame her… But he had loved her… he did love her…

'*Our separation is transitory. I can only hope that through the fire of my love I live on in your heart…*'

What he would give for Annie to hold him in her arms. He tucks a hand under his pillow and feels there his wife's slim book, *Shadow is a Colour as Light is*, as cool and dry as her own hand.

Jeffrey lies on his bed, quite, quite still. He breathes deeply, calmly. He has taken to lying down with Walter when he sleeps, though Jeffrey does not always fall asleep himself. He keeps his father's bedroom on permanent display so as to be always next to him, stares for hours at Walter's desiccated and wizened body. His hair all gone, so shrunken he barely registers on screen, he is a ghost already.

Sometimes, he alternates between guarding Walter and gaming; long-form quest games being his preference, projecting himself into those alternative worlds to while away the indistinct waiting time. He plays so long he enters into another kind of meditative state, projecting himself into the alternative worlds of his father's mind, merging with scenes that replay on the screens, or in his imagination, visions Jeffrey makes up, like he's writing his own Walter Yeung fanfic, in which he himself appears.

In this present moment's half-vision, half dream, the clattering whirr of his desk fan becomes the motor of a huge sliding door, which is the entrance to the Yeung family mausoleum. His inner camera pulls back and he watches his avatar padding barefoot across a vast stone floor.

It's a scene from countless games and movie spin-offs; the inside of some ancient catacomb containing sought after treasure but fraught with many dangers. But where are Jeffrey's weapons?

He has none, but a flaming torch materialises in his hand and, emboldened, he slinks through unchartered space until he stops at another opening, a black hole through which he must enter.

He passes through the doorway to find a body's form laid out on a grandly ornate catafalque, a sheet of midnight-blue velvet covering it. Jeffrey pulls the sheet away to reveal his father's face, restored to plump health below his shock of thick grey hair, re-grown.

Suddenly, Walter's eyes flick open and Jeffrey jumps back. "Father!"

As the echo of his cry falls away, a call comes from somewhere else inside the space; a mellow, soft voice he doesn't recognise but seems to know. "Jeffrey? Jeffrey?"

He pans round and creeps further into the dark, the torch lighting a halo of ground around his feet.

Eventually, a wall emerges from the bluey-black void before him. It is lined with carved niches and, in one of them lies a small body shrouded in what appears to be a white tablecloth. Beside the niche, a printed label of the kind you might find on an art gallery wall. It reads, *Walter Yeung Jr. (1988-1990)*.

Jeffrey pulls back. So these are the trials to be faced, the tribulations to overcome, the battles fought, all while unarmed. The next niche along contains another, adult, body, this one uncovered but whose shape he can barely make out. He brings up the torch to read its own label: *Gor Gor (1956 - 2003)*.

He releases a huge sigh, strong enough to extinguish the torch he is holding plunging him into pitch darkness. Before he descends into panic, a dim light source glows from a niche above those of his two elder brothers — the real, and the wished for. He is able to make out a figure slowly rising out of a dense covering of flowers that lift up and fall away until his mother is standing there, smiling. She comes to him then, hugs him tight in her arms.

It's over too soon. She vanishes and his arms tingle with the residue of her hold. It is time to leave, but where, he thinks, where is the hidden treasure? There is always a treasure. Oh, it was that hug, of course...

He retreats through the space, back towards his father's corpse. There is light this time, rows and rows of torches illuminating the tomb. Walter's eyes are closed and he appears to be at rest.

But Jeffrey spots something bulky and square beneath the midnight-blue sheet that he hadn't been aware of earlier. What's this — bonus treasure?

He pulls the midnight-blue cover away and it pools on the floor. His father's arms are crossed over his torso, gripping a small gilded frame. Jeffrey peers down at the obscured canvas, but can't make it out.

He pulls and pulls at Walter's arms until, at last, one stiffened limb falls away and there is Cézanne's *Still Life with Apples and Jug*, his mother's favourite painting.

Jeffrey springs up from the bed, his heart pounding with the clarity of his vision. He couldn't have planned it better himself.

Sophie, New York — 2010

Sophie came to a halt on the Met's grand staircase, the one leading up from the Great Hall. She was experiencing a strange kind of déjà vu, or was it a memory? An image flash triggered by another sense, but she couldn't put her finger on what; maybe the metal sensuality of the banister under her hand, or the heady smell from the spectacular arrangement of flowers that drifted down to her, or the sandpapery shuffling sound her pumps made on the stone steps, or... no, she couldn't yet figure it out.

Joel came back from the bathroom, had been feeling unwell, he said, and climbed the stairs. He looked pale, fragile, grey round the eyes, and the front of his hair was slicked across his forehead from splashing water on his face. She should ask if he was feeling better, but such enquiries could open up into all kinds of mess and she was feeling pretty brittle herself right now.

As he drew level, she said, "Remember when he came to the exhibit?" nodding towards the giant poster hanging above the main ticket desk. There was Marius Woolf, imposed onto a backdrop of Mont Sainte-Victoire in darkly brooding profile, advertising the movie tie-in ticket deal. "Christa had to Google him when his agent confirmed, because she'd invited so many people she could barely remember who was who. When we saw that LaChapelle photo-shoot we screamed! Him all oiled-up by the motel pool in his satin kick-boxing shorts like that…"

Christa had even used one of those vivid, hyper-real images — Marius lying naked on an inflatable lounger, floating in the blue-green pool itself — as her screensaver, for a while, and, in the run up to the exhibit, their nerves and excitement mounting, his delicious ass became a reference point for anything they considered remotely praiseworthy or wonderful.

"When he arrived we weren't sure it was really him, because he looked so different. Now he ends up starring as my favourite painter in a movie. It's so weird, right?"

Joel didn't answer. He still looked dizzy, as if unsure where, or who, he was. "Do you really want to go do this?" she asked him. "Are you sure you're up to a movie?"

Despite his fragile appearance, his response was clear and certain. "Sure I am, Soph. I'd love to see it with you. C'mon, course I would." He put on a deep, blockbuster-movie-trailer-voice: "*Marius Woolf is Paul Cézanne.*" It was a relief to see him joke. "I do remember that we lived off his money for two whole years," he added with a queasy smile. "Christ knows I couldn't provide for us after my dad cut me off. My skill set wasn't exactly prodigious."

She'd been anxious about letting those paintings go, at the thought of someone else owning her self-portraits. When she'd told Christa she wanted to keep *Sophie #1* for herself they were worried the deal might fall through if he couldn't have them all, but the memory of how super nice he was about this meant she became aware of Joel's centering of his own feelings, yet again, in the story of her success.

"And do you also remember that I made a choice, Joel, to use that money to focus on my painting? You would finish your first collection, we agreed, which you did. *And* it got published. I've no regrets about where that money went, and if it was the same situation in reverse we wouldn't even be having this conversation."

"You're right, Soph," Joel said. "I'm sorry. I'm... I don't know. Sorry. Let's keep going."

She'd become better at challenging the pull of his vulnerability, though her own strength confused her because it was fragile too. She could challenge him like this, but immediately felt guilty for it and, on top of that, there was just the sheer, urgent drama of Imogen's needs and thinking what was best for her now that Joel was better, now she knew the cause of everything that had happened.

It was difficult resisting the pressure from all sides; from her mom and dad who, every phone call these days, were urging her to give him one more try, for Immy's sake, or from the friends who encouraged her to go it alone, all ready to print their *Sophie #1* t-shirts and cheer her into the future, and those few much closer to her, like Christa, who knew the situation's complexities and what a shambles she was, people who'd care for her no matter what she decided, but who she didn't want to let down, nevertheless. How to know what's right in the face of all that?

"At least if the movie's dire we'll have seen the paintings again," Sophie said, by way of conciliation.

They were at the top of the stairs by now and Joel stopped and gazed to the bottom. Sophie was afraid all of a sudden that he was going to launch himself into the air, imagined his broken body sprawled on the stone ground below. The déjà vu returned, and she felt, vividly, Joel pulling her down with him, shattering her.

"When I was a kid," he said, "our staircase at home looked to me as big as this one. I was made to sit at the top for hours, totally quiet and absolutely still. It was one of my punishments. I'd listen to my father's

181

friends and business associates, his secretary and his PA, all moving around and talking to each other. They didn't know I was there — I was invisible — and I found I could project myself into them if I tried hard enough."

They'd been together a while before Sophie realised exactly how wealthy Joel's father was, and then how much Joel despised him. The first time Sophie met his father, she sensed a vibration emanating when he held her hand for too long, as if he was trying to consume her, taunting Joel through her, intimating that he could take her if he wanted. "Oh she's a fiery one, Poop," was what he said when she'd pulled away. She was glad when Joel and his dad finally split for good, though that relief didn't last long because it took the lid of everything.

"The only time I kind of liked my dad," Joel said, "was when we weren't in the same room, but I could still hear him. I liked to know he was there but now I know it was like monitoring a snake. If he was going to attack I needed to know exactly what was coming."

Where was this all coming from today, Sophie wondered. Should she be worried? He wasn't agitated, or angry, looking everywhere except at her. She didn't think he was playing one of his past games.

He moved on into the light-bathed corridor filled with the Rodin sculptures whose dark bronze greedily absorbed the atrium's diffuse light, and Sophie followed. They drifted together through the nineteenth century galleries, as they had done many times before. It felt as if no time at all had passed since they were last here, despite everything that had happened since. Still, now that they were speaking again, there was a whole future ahead of awkward meetings in nice places, which they'd never escape, linked as they were and always would be by their daughter. People moved on, apparently, incredibly, which was as unimaginable to her as inhabiting a different body, being another person entirely.

Joel started again, his words floating through the high space right up to the glass atrium at the top. "Those rare times when he seemed to like me, he'd call me into his study and allow me to sit and do my schoolwork beside him. There were days when he'd proclaim himself Emperor and get me to make chains of coloured paper to place around his neck." He acted out the ghostly assembling of the paper chains, and then solemnly mimed his father's coronation.

"It was when my father didn't like me that I was confined to my bedroom. It could last weeks — *weeks* — my food delivered on trays left outside the door, the adjoining bathroom the furthest I was allowed to venture. I'd be desperate. When you're that age, weeks is an eternity."

Sophie had learned never to bring his father up in conversation herself but, when Joel wanted to, it was best to just let him speak without any comment. What would she have said anyway, about the terrible things he'd done? His circular ruminations, these variations on a theme, made her sure there was unexplored, inarticulated poetry in these episodes. He even used his poetry reading voice when telling the stories — detached and strangely dreamy, in language that was careful, thoughtful. Joel had never written anything about his father that she knew of, was avoiding the thing he needed to write about, and that's why he was unable to write anything. But she couldn't say anything about that, either.

Like all the questions she'd had at the start of their relationship, about his mom's disappearance when Joel was just five years old, these words she might say evaporated in the white heat of his pain and she couldn't persevere with him as a project.

During one of their worst arguments, she'd repeated those questions — "What did your dad do to make her leave? How can someone just vanish these days? Why didn't she take you with her?" — but with venom that time, not concern. She told him that, no matter how much she loved him she would never have married him if she'd known what he was. Though she thinks it was the worst thing she's ever said to anyone, Joel had simply nodded in agreement with all of it.

They arrived, finally, at the main Cézanne room. Sophie had thought to go to Hortense immediately but seeing her there she was confronted by a loss of nerve. She liked the Belgian actress who'd been cast to play her, but was perturbed at the prospect of seeing her old friend made flesh, embodied beyond the voice that existed in her head, still, years after her study of these portraits had ended. Their communion had intensified during Sophie's worst times. She was more Hortense than she wanted to be and didn't want to see herself in those portraits just now.

As Joel came in behind her, she went instead to *Still Life with Apples and a Pot of Primroses*, immersed herself in the radiant background, drew nearer to bathe in its complex, shimmering surface of delicate greens and blues. Sophie wouldn't play the long-suffering wife, but was feeling and fearing the impulse to try again with him. Though she didn't believe it was her job to heal or save him (where did these words come from?) her inability to do so was something she couldn't help see as a great failure on her part, while hating herself for thinking that way.

She perceived a streak of pink flashing across the blue, and then more streaks, vibrating. She'd never experienced this before; the blue and pink and green passing through and into her like waves of light, tuning her in to its energy, allowing her to hear clearly what she had strained to hear before now: this heart's singing, calling to the gallery, to Sophie and Joel, the whole world, challenging them all to accept its song. Would she ever make anything as marvellous as this? It seemed to ask so many questions. Any risk she might take, any words she eventually said, could not go as badly as anything that had already passed between them.

As Joel sat on the bench in front of Hortense she focused on the table covered with its white crumpled cloth and flowering pot plant with dark green leaves, the apples and their astonishing layers of dark reds and greens and browns, over purple, or navy blue, or a brighter green, each one its own entire still life.

She counted them; twenty-two, some bunched together, others lined in a row, a few nestling singly in the white tablecloth that rose above them in mountainous ridges, the white fabric hardly ever plain white at all but reflecting the blue-green-pink background, or purple and green in the folds and creases that formed the landscape — the folds undulating hills, the apples tucked amongst the creases like village houses and, towering above everything, the dark spread leaves of the plant were open arms, like flying, or falling, both, then her own arms waiting to receive their child, and him.

You don't get many chances to put things right. Couldn't they just say sorry to each other and start over? Would that be enough. Yes, they could say that. She could say that.

Nick, Liverpool — 2008

The woman being killed is lying face up on the ground. Her mouth is open, still, the other woman still bent over, pressing down on her shoulders. The murderer has not brought down his arm, which is raised, as before, gripping the knife.

The two girls are still there too, the one in the apple green Puffa jacket, and her friend sitting on the floor, as focused on their drawing as Nick was on his.

He'll not hurt them, or himself. He'll not hurt Maria who he can see coming in. He grips the knife tightly and approaches the painting. He's not in a car park watching a man he loved and hated burn to death. He can't save Jimmy, so he'll save the woman in the picture.

Maria's voice comes floating through, gently, insistently — "Nick? Nick, love? Nick?" — but he won't look because if he sees her he might lose his nerve.

He lifts his arm and takes a step forward, aiming for the man whose arm is up like his, the murderer. His focus shifts and he sees himself reflected in the protective glass. The oily-bluey-black of the background's void paints the glass surface the same colour as the scorched windows of Jimmy's car that Nick saw himself reflected in as he burned.

The knife won't break through the glass, Nick realises. It's just a stupid little fruit knife. He could curl up on the floor below the painting and sleep, but is trapped in the glass, furiously mute, caught in the violence that he can't not remember, that he can't break out of. His aching arm drops. It burns too.

Seeing his shoulders slump, his head bowed, Maria treads softly towards him. He'll be alright. He's still got the knife but she doesn't think the painting, the one she'd told him to come and see, is in danger any more. What was she thinking? She should've known better. "Nick? Nick, love?"

He looks up and a scene projects itself onto the charcoal-coloured glass, of Jimmy taking a swing at him, in the kitchen, when he was just a boy, and his fist catching Nick on the shoulder, so that he fell back against the electric hob, burning his arm, badly. They couldn't take him to hospital because the nurses might have asked him questions, and he'd always told everyone, even Maria, that the scars were from landing on his mum's curling tongs one time, when he'd been bouncing up and down on the bed. If Nick told Maria this story now she might stay. The woman's voice comes again from the painting: *No, she won't stay.*

She won't say his name again because he's not responding, but will take some more steps towards him and lead him away from the painting and down the stairs, because the security guy will probably be here any second and she doesn't want Nick to get into trouble, so she has to move quickly.

Maria comes beside him and puts her hand on his shoulder and, burned by the touch, Nick jerks away and doesn't even see her when he swings round and his hand comes up from his side and stabs the knife in her belly.

188

It wasn't Jimmy's hand on him, it was Maria's hand, and now her mouth is open in the same small black hollow as the woman lying on the ground, being killed.

Maria frowns, bites her bottom lip as she doubles over and falls, curled up beneath the painting.

There's screams from in the room, from the girls, that let the air out, and it's not right, but what has he done?

There's blood on the floor and the fruit knife and his hand are covered in blood, and the pool of blood on the floor is getting bigger, and it's Maria's blood.

The security guard who ran in when he heard the screams has his hands out towards Nick, and he looks scared, Nick thinks, and the girl in the apple green Puffa jacket is holding her friend and not letting her look and he hopes to God she didn't see what he's done, because if she did he's ruined her whole bloody life for her, and he hates himself for doing that.

Nick looks to the painting. Nothing's changed. He couldn't do it.

He strides towards the security guard who he knows won't stop him because he's too scared and has never had to deal with anything like this before. He holds out the knife and the guard takes it quietly from him. He hopes they get to Maria soon, who's lying on the floor, holding her stomach, legs wheeling slowly in the spreading pool of blood. She'll be alright, won't she?

Nick thinks he can make it over the railing but he'll have to run hard if he's to do it in one go and he has all the energy he needs now, having decided.

He runs and gets the stride just right so that his foot lands firm on the railing when he jumps and launches himself into the air and he sees, in the café below, the woman serving the tea and cakes put a hand

189

over her mouth as she looks up at him, reaching towards him with her other hand, red raw from the hot washing-up water, and, as he plunges down, he's sorry that she'll have to clean up after him.

Sophie & Joel, New York — 2010

Joel was reading that Cézanne's friends used to call his wife 'La Boule', the ball-and-chain, and even he used this cruel nickname for her sometimes. He'd leave her alone a lot of the time, and his mother and sister then treated her with open hostility, certain she was trying to get her hands on the family money. Joel's dad had said the same thing to him about Sophie once, the last time they ever spoke.

He was sitting with Sophie's copy of Annie Yeung's book resting open on his lap, in front of the two portraits of Madame Cézanne. In one, Joel thought, Cézanne had hardly painted a woman at all. The fireplace, the chair, the curtains, all dominated and the shapes and configuration of the red dress she wore seemed more vital to him than the person inside it, as if it was only her formal solidity that fascinated him and not her body at all. He may as well have been painting his mountain.

But the other painting, the one of her sitting on a terrace in front of flowers, had some human warmth in it, some affection. This was definitely a portrait of a real woman, her tenderly expressive face that of a loved one, the body she inhabited a living body, shapely and slender-waisted, not an effigy wrapped and trapped in red fabric.

Joel's eyes flitted between the two, assessing the degrees of melancholy with which she regarded him, and he felt scrutinised by her in turn. He felt he was witnessing a wife and husband, subject and artist, surveying each other across an unbridgeable gulf, and she, looking out at Joel, was seeing the same. Had they felt much love for each other?

He flicked through the book, both in search of an answer and to avoid the question being bounced back at him, but one of Sophie's marginal scribbles stopped him. In light blue pencil, she'd written 'Cézanne's fear of touch', beside a sentence of Annie Yeung's text, itself underlined in darker blue:

Her hands contained memories, emotions, thoughts, all of which her husband felt unable to portray, to represent, or which, perhaps, he actively sought to erase.

Joel looked up to examine those hands and realised that they were, in both cases, only sketched out or obscured, barely there. He thought of Sophie's hands at the time they were first dating. Her bitten-down fingernails, and the bruised looking knuckles caused, she'd told him, by paint embedded in the lines there that she couldn't get out without scrubbing hard and she couldn't be bothered most of the time. She'd never grown her nails into those talons in her early self-portraits, the ones owned now by Marius Woolf. Except for *Sophie #1*, which he'd not seen for quite some time, given it hung above Sophie's bed.

He'd even begun a poem about her hands once, initially thought she craved those dripping red talons for herself, but gave it up when she said how uneasy she was at the notion of him interpreting her. He turned to look for her and found her haloed by the bright blue background of the still life, her shoulders encircled by apples and engulfed in pink flowers. One hand was covering her mouth, the other placed on her hip, her arm wrapped around her waist.

Those formerly agitated hands were cleaner and calmer these days, just as his own were becoming more sullied and useless, and she'd stopped biting her nails when Immy was just a few weeks old, just like he'd quit his occasional smoking the moment Sophie got pregnant. Oh, and that ring she used to wear, the one with the glass eye that matched her own, she'd stopped wearing that around the same time.

Sophie sensed Joel staring at her, but stayed in the company of the still life a while longer. She'd found Immy in this canvas already, as an apple nestled between the folds of tablecloth, then there too, suddenly, the pot of primroses was Joel, his arms stretched out wide over them. After everything he'd put her through she couldn't help but see him. He'd started to appear in her recent work, too; a shadowy figure in the background, sometimes protective, sometimes looming, just like here. Threatening, even. It was a compulsion, outside her control, as if she wanted his presence while also needing to erase it.

This was the moment to go to him, she felt, but she feared facing Hortense's questioning gaze. She'd only ask Sophie where she's been and why they haven't spoken these last few months. But she was going to need to put all her fears aside today.

As she approached Joel, she noticed he was thumbing through a book. With a churning bewilderment she realised what it was and reached out. "Where did you find it! We looked all over, Joel, didn't we?"

He could pretend he'd only recently found it, but didn't want to lie, not today. "It — it wasn't really lost, Soph," he told her. "I only said it was. I wanted to keep it."

"To keep it…?" He was holding the precious book out to her to take, but she remained a few paces distant from him. "Joel! You knew how much this book means to me. I was frantic about it."

"I'm really sorry, Soph. Don't be angry. Yes, I know, of course I do — it wasn't that I wanted to steal it. I just couldn't stand not having it. When you suggested we go see this movie, I was so psyched about doing that together, and coming here with you again… I guess I had an attack of conscience. I knew I had to give it back. I was wrong to keep it."

"You couldn't stand not having it?" She scrutinised him with the same tilted head, the same inquisitive sadness, as Cézanne's wife sitting on her terrace. Both expressions, the painted and the real, pressed for an explanation.

"It's your annotations, you see? Reading them made me feel you were still around. I was reading one just now, when you were over there with the apples and flowers, and it's like you're speaking directly into my head. You've written something here," he said, pointing to the marked page. "What does it mean?"

She knew he wanted to bring her round, make her like him again and was beyond wary, thought she might hate him, but when she stepped forward and took the book from him her whole body loosened. "My fingers remember the book," she said, breaking into surprised laughter. "I can feel it. They remember…" She slumped down onto the bench next to him.

Joel's hands were tingling after releasing hold of it. He hadn't realised how hard he was gripping. To compensate, he slotted one hand into the pocket where he kept the red and gold pencil stub, all that remained from the box she'd presented to him that first time in Caffe Reggio. He held it stable this time, no jabbing himself with it, like in the park.

The answer to his question contained a story, and Sophie would tell it to him without fear, without worrying how it might make him feel, because it wasn't his. Not every story was his. She'd do it the best way she could; honestly and directly.

"Cézanne was bullied, really bad, at school. One time, he was about fourteen, another boy snuck up behind him and kicked him so hard in the ass he fell down a whole flight of stairs. After that, he developed a — a horror — of physical contact of any kind, which only got worse throughout his life."

The peculiar déjà vu returned to disorient her and she saw, then felt, herself lying at the bottom of the Met's grand staircase, her body smashed into a thousand crystalline pieces. She saw too, astonishingly, Joel's inky ass jeans from their first meeting, but the dark blue stain was a bruise, this time, a mark of all the violence ever done to him. She pressed a finger and thumb against the bridge of her nose. No, she didn't hate him.

"Is something wrong, Soph? You okay?" Joel asked. His impulse was to put his arm around her, but he resisted.

Sophie straightened up, nodded, "I'm okay," and re-settled herself. "Imagine being married to someone who can't bear to be touched." She thrust the book towards the portraits. "Poor Hortense."

"Why did she stay with him?" he asked.

"Well, what were her choices? I mean, she had no profession, besides bookbinding, or occasional modelling, and she wouldn't go back to any of that. Though, I guess... I guess she loved him. At the start at least. They were both lonely, and they found each other. He could have abandoned her when she got pregnant — it wouldn't have been so unusual among their set — but he didn't. He stayed with her. At least he has that in the plus column. And he adored their son — little Paul. She wasn't cut out to be an artist's wife, I think. Despite his moods, his total lack of social skills and refusal to compromise, they stuck together."

195

This speech had enabled her to take some deep breaths, and she felt calmer, lighter. "See those metal tongs beside the fireplace?" She pointed to the red dress painting "She must've wanted to take them up and bash his brains out sometimes. I know I would. Still, being looked at by Paul Cézanne the same way he looked at an apple, or a mountain, is no small thing. It's not the life I'd want, but I guess you already know that." She bumped shoulders with him, jokingly.

He was forgiven, he thought, they were making a truce. No, that wasn't right. He didn't deserve it. He was using fragments of information gathered from what he'd read in her book, acting as if he didn't know anything about the Cézannes' marriage, to deliberately draw Sophie back towards him. It was monstrous and the flashing impulse to jab himself resurfaced. He sat with it for a few seconds, until it faded.

"…hated himself a lot of the time," Sophie was saying, "and completely trapped by bitterness and frustration, though some people did love him, strangely. I think he loved his male friends the most, inseparable, until Zola's betrayal that is. I think this stuff's in the movie from what I've heard. It still amazes me that he was able to move away from his torment and inner violence — well, not completely — but that he was able to do all this." She swept her arm around the room, enveloping the apples, the primroses, the mountain, everything on display.

He didn't react to her all-encompassing gesture, and his continued silent scrutiny of the drawing unnerved and irritated her — Hortense was hers, like Annie's book was hers. It felt so good to hold it again, to inhale its slight perfumed mustiness.

"Let me show you something," she said.

She'd found the drawing she was looking for, a simple pencil and watercolour sketch of a cluster of flowers and some partially painted leaves. To the right, smaller and rendered in pencil lines only, was a beautiful study of a woman's head, resting on a pillow. She looked like she'd just woken up and turned to her husband at that tranquil moment of waking. A few light strands of hair had come loose from her perfect centre parting and rested on her brow.

"When I first saw this I thought it was one of the most beautiful things he ever did. All this delicacy and lightness." She planted a finger on the caption, *Madame Cézanne with Hortensias, 1885.* "But she's always Madame Cézanne, isn't she — on these labels and in these books? Hardly anyone knows what her real name was, even when it would make more sense to tell you. He must have drawn those particular flowers — hortensias — to reference her".

Joel focused on the restful gaze looking out from the page. It was hard to credit this as the same woman sitting in front of them. Cézanne was looking at someone he truly loved, it was certain, and so was she looking back at him — Joel felt it. But still love hadn't been enough to make them happy.

"For someone whose manner was so antisocial and so, so *brutish.*" Sophie continued, "to capture her like this... maybe that pure oval face was what he loved; the perfect shape of it." Just then, a child's voice called out across the gallery "Flower!"

Sophie turned and saw a woman with a buggy smiling across at them. Her kid, all twisted round in the straps, was waving at Joel with a crumpled piece of paper and Joel waved back.

Sophie was rippled by a cold shiver, imagined him with this woman, who had a child with him. He had another life, without her. The woman's gentle smile and small nod towards Joel confirmed it "Who — who's that?" she was able to ask.

"Oh, I don't know. I met them in the park while I was waiting for you. The little guy was acting up so I did a drawing for him — well, a pencil rubbing actually, of a flower carved into the bench. See it?" he said, "in his hand? I think he likes it."

It seemed he'd conjured them, somehow, right then, to show Sophie he wasn't a bad man at all. She understands now, that mom, seeing him and Sophie together, why he was peculiar before. Why life is difficult for him right now. She exonerated him, too, for unnerving her by ranting at nothing. He intuited all this and was immediately grateful.

Sophie watched as the woman passed through the space, her kid still waving his happy paper at Joel. A low, rhythmic voice was saying something about *Cézanne's questions… his questioning of whoever was looking.* A tall, thoughtful-looking museum guide with heavy spectacles and a grey linen scarf furled around his neck was standing in front of a gorgeous landscape. Constructed of pale lozenges of green, orange, blue and white, a tour group were gazing at it with varying degrees of interest.

Joel pulled himself up from the bench and moved towards *Still Life With Apples and a Pot of Primroses.* He scrutinised its mountain of white cloth, the fruit and flowers and glorious blue, all its dizzying colours, as Sophie had. He had to approach it — her — obliquely, not head on, had to direct the action so that anything decided today would seem like Sophie's decision.

He felt her join him, at his side. He couldn't afford to make the wrong move. A life can be totally transformed in a moment by that kind of mistake, he knew — like the day he'd told her he had to leave them. How might their lives have ended up if he'd never spoken those words? They might still be together, as a family. Were things really as simple as all that; an act of senseless violence on a staircase, painting a woman in a red dress or a blue dress, the difference between speaking and not speaking?

"The whole thing's about to give way," Joel said. "Have you noticed?

The table's going to topple over, and those apples are going to roll right out of the frame — the flowerpot will smash to pieces on the floor. All the objects existing at the same time, in the same space, but it's impossible, physically, seeing them from different angles all at once like this — and yet here they are, all held together by him, in their own beautiful, fragmented world."

Sophie had never heard him speak about Cézanne this way before. If you could learn anything from these paintings, she thought, it wouldn't only be from the questions they posed, but from what was spoken in front of them, the words people said to each other about them, which were really words about themselves.

"He knows how to push it to the limit, that's for sure," she responded. "It could all break down but he manages to make the foundations solid with colours, and through form. He's just about preventing the whole world he's created from collapsing."

"It's like being shown what it means to be human," Joel said. "You can kind of accept the imbalances because — the whole thing — just — *works*."

She said, "He's not trying to impress you with, you know, 'This fruit's so lifelike you could bite into it', or, 'Go ahead, smell these realistic flowers'. He's making a different statement about reality. He's not trying to capture the transitory moment either. He's more into setting down permanence, or appealing for it to arise."

Sophie recalled the strange sensation of having shattered she'd felt earlier, and of the effort required in putting herself back together. Of putting her and Joel back together.

"Even though Mont Sainte-Victoire never changes, each time he paints it, it's different. Like the portraits of Hortense are different. What's he really painting when he paints an apple, or the mountain?

What's he painting when he paints his wife? He's painting himself. That's what changes."

As she was speaking, Joel could heard another voice, laid on top of hers, not low and rhythmic, like that museum guide, but light and urgent, as the little boy's — *Speak to her. Go on, speak to her!* Was he here again?

No — it was the small pink primroses, he realised, crying out, and then the apples, in which Cézanne had placed a total affirmation of life, a life in which anything and everything was possible, joined in and chorused: *Say what's true, Say what's true, Say what's true…*

You can't get it right all the time but you can get it right some of the time. You can put some things right. *He* can. He can reach out to her. He can speak.

"Soph, I wanted to — to apologise — for the way I am. I've been scared my whole fucking life. I kept so much from you and that made me even more scared — if I even tried to tell you half the things I've kept back… but we can't let ourselves end up like them."

It was possible to become trapped in mute frustration, or worse, bitterness that showed itself in violently fragmented, scribbled hands. What if he was a clever, cynical, manipulating bully, just like his dad, tricking her into loving him? But he had to give her more credit. She was stronger and cleverer and better than that.

But was he just using the same techniques he'd learned to bring his father round? Softening the mood and soothing a situation, which was really a manipulation, even when his feelings were genuine and good. He didn't know any other way to be and he hated himself for it.

Then the pencil jabbing — he felt the jabbing again — and thrust his useless, non-writing hand into his pocket and gripped the pencil there, but it couldn't hold him together as it usually did, the world falling apart just as he'd foreseen, the table collapsing, the pot smashing on the floor, the apples scattering and tumbling out of the frame.

The cloth was smothering, suffocating him — he felt a cry rise in his throat — he would empty out all the words trapped inside.

Then, one of the apples dropped into his hand. He'd caught it, small, dry, and perfect, when it rolled towards him.

He looked down to examine it and there, instead, resting in his hand, was Sophie's hand.

J-P, Liverpool — 2008

J-P watched Marius through the viewer, rehearsing his gestures, movement, and expressions. Following J-P's instructions, the make-up technician had sallowed his face, applied pale violet shadows under his eyes, and created visible cracks on his lips. All this, along with the grubbing up of his neck and collar, the greased and dirtied hair, paint-streaked, unwashed hands, painted a picture of Paul's neglect and unease.

First, they'd film him stalking and storming through Paris, then shoot his awkward reaction to Émile shouting to him from the carriage, followed by Paul's reluctant embrace of his closest friend. In the flashback J-P had written, to explain Paul's fear of touch, he conflates the young Paul being kicked down the school stairs with their first meeting, when Émile had intervened in a separate episode of bullying. In the film version of their story, this moment marks the beginning of them as the Inseparables, and that's all that matters.

They had a few minutes to go before shooting, so J-P tried Maria's mobile again. She already felt like a friend, and he wanted to tell her what he'd decided, about his dad.

He couldn't remember the last time he'd talked so openly than with her last night, over dinner. J-P knew Maria had spied their hands touching in the car that ferried him and Marius from the airport that first day. She'd known about them the whole week and not said a word until he brought it up himself, which meant she could be trusted. When she answered the phone, J-P heard a background clamour and someone shouting before the call got dropped. She must be busy on set, organising everything, which she was so good at. She was going to be a great P.A.

They'd all be in New York together first, before heading over to L.A. for J-P to make a start on the edit. Last night, he'd told Maria about his first time there. He'd won an award at film school; a six-month postgrad course at NYFA, all paid for, with flights and accommodation included. Walking round the Metropolitan Museum, soaking it all in, he'd come across a painting of some apples and a pot of pink primroses set against a joyous blue-green background.

When he'd read the label and saw it was by Cézanne he was flooded with missing his mum, who died when he was eleven. "It made me cry, like properly cry, for the first time in ages."

He'd asked himself why, of all the pictures in the Met, it should be a painting of apples and flowers that would release those emotions in him, even before he knew who'd made it. And he asked the painting those questions too, was continuing to do so, in his film, trying to make sense of how paintings live on in the world, speaking beyond their intention to the many thousands of people who look at them every day. Of course, he'd worried these questions were of no interest to anyone but himself except here he was, years later, standing outside the Walker where it all really started, making his film.

J-P told the story of how his dad would take him to the Royal when his mum was having her chemo because he insisted on going with them. His mum agreed as long as he didn't wait in the hospital. "It's dead time, love," she'd say. "Go and do something nice instead."

They'd go round the city centre until the call came to go and pick her up and, one rainy afternoon his dad had taken him to the Walker Art Gallery, for something a bit different. "He trailed after me as I wandered around," J-P said, "looking at picture after picture, and that's when I first saw *The Murder*. He tried to move us on but I couldn't take my eyes off it. I had questions he couldn't answer — What was happening, Why was it so dark, Who were the people in it and who'd make a thing like that?"

That afternoon, he took his mum her cup of tea in bed and heard his dad telling her how weird he thought it was for a ten year old to like this ugly, creepy painting so much.

His mum laughed softly, and said "He's funny that one."

And then his dad said, "Morbid more like."

"Maybe it's something to do with what's happening to me," his mum suggested. "We should try talking to him about it."

J-P took the tea in and his mum pulled herself up to sitting. "There's my lad," she said. "Your dad's just been describing the picture you liked. Will you tell me about it?"

"I can't remember now exactly what words I used," he told Maria, "but I felt the killer's white shirt flying up at the back, then holding the knife and looking into the woman's open mouth and being scared by the other woman, goading me on. It was like I was in the painting, not looking at it. But I couldn't say that. I didn't know how to. I think I was scared of being judged, of being loved less because of liking such a horrible thing."

His mum was propped up on her pillow, cradling the tea in her lap. His dad's words about him went round and round in his head and when he'd finished his own description his mum simply said, "I'll go and see it with you, once my bones are better."

J-P thought he might cry then, his voice shaky and high as he told how his mum got admitted to the Royal the next week and he and his dad went up there every day, after school. Eventually, she was moved into her own room. One time, the doctor came in and asked to talk to his dad on his own and as they were going out into the corridor he heard the doctor say, "She's had a bad night."

His mum was curled up in bed, holding her stomach, frowning, eyes closed, mouth open a little and he'd thought, she looks like the woman in the painting — the one being killed — "and that was when I realised she wasn't going to get any better," he said.

He'd sat down on the bed next to her, which roused her and she opened her eyes, reached out to squeeze his hand and whispered, "I just want to go somewhere nice." Maria had put her hand in his then, and she too was all trembling and teary.

"Oh Maria, love," J-P said. "I didn't mean to upset *you*."

She'd laughed huskily and wiped her eyes on her napkin. "It's not your fault. It's… an emotional night. My life's about to change, that's all."

Truth be told, Maria reminded him of his mum. Being back in Liverpool meant he was thinking about her all the time as it was. The job he'd offered her was difficult for her to accept, he could tell. She wanted this opportunity, but she was nervous, doubtful, scared of taking chances when they were offered. It only made him more determined to help Maria realise her dreams in a way that he'd never been able to do for his mum, who'd wanted to design her own clothes, maybe open a shop, but never had the chance or the money, and was only thirty-five when the cancer took her.

To change the subject, and more than a few glasses of prosecco in, J-P had told her how he and Marius first met at Cannes before getting it together in L.A. He plunged in to the story of collecting and saving the LaChapelle and *Cosmo* photos, and the film stills, which he'd never said out loud before. It was such a relief he only then realised the amount of pressure he'd been putting his relationship under. "I'm going to delete them all," he declared, "as soon as I get a spare bloody moment. I don't need them anymore, do I? I've got the real thing." They clinked glasses at that.

His needing Maria there, now, standing next to him on set, made him realise he was doing the same thing with her as he'd done to Marius. He was conflating his image of his mum with his perception of her. This sudden concern wouldn't stop him. She was her own person, after all, and she'd be great to have around. He'd have his own band of Inseparables. Maria and Marius, Marius and Maria; it was going to be perfect.

He was about to get the Assistant Director to call quiet on the set but Marius suddenly gestured at him to come over. J-P went to him, put an arm around his shoulder and led him away behind one of the columns of St. George's Hall. "What is it?"

"J-P, listen — I — there's something I need to say and I know I shouldn't hold things up like this, but — I want you to know that I think you're doing a great job. I don't think I've said that to you before now, not explicitly. Take it from me, this is your movie and you wrote a great fucking script and whatever happens, in the future, don't let me, or anyone else, take that away from you. Okay?"

"Marius... what?"

"I love you, you know that?"

"Yes, I think so." J-P lowered his voice, just in case. "And I love you."

Marius nodded, but he was teary, and put his hand on the side of J-P's. The gesture felt awkward, troubled. He was still caught up rehearsing Paul, J-P thought. Wasn't quite himself.

They stepped out from behind the column and Marius called out, loud as he could, "I fucking love this guy!" A ragged cheer went up from the crew, no doubt glad that whatever pep talk they'd been giving each other had worked and they could just get on with it.

J-P caught sight of the extra again, the one who reminded him of his dad. Now that he knew it wasn't him, J-P's sharp anxiety had been replaced by blunt guilt, not just for how he was acting now towards his dad, but all that had brought him to this. He knew he had to put it right, somehow.

There weren't answers to the questions of painting and his film had no great climactic resolution as a result. The final scene was just Cézanne walking through the fields at Aix-en-Provençe at the end, his satchel and canvas on his back. Cézanne had shown him it was possible to make something beautiful out of your difficulties, to work hard at beauty until it sings out at you and makes you cry for reasons you don't understand.

The true backstory, the one underneath everything else, underneath his high-blown talk of making a work of art that replicated Cézanne's technique of multiple perspectives, underneath experimenting with repeated scenes from different viewpoints, creating a sense of a whole from variations on visual themes, was the simple story of a man trying to make sense of what it means to be a human being, alive in the world, which was his story, Paul's story, his dad's story.

He waited for the noise to die down, for everyone to settle. Marius was dabbing at his eyes, dancing on his toes. He seemed manic but that only energised J-P too.

"Okay," J-P shouted. "We're ready to go!"

The AD was about to step forward with her clapperboard when they all heard the ambulances wailing — two of them — going towards the Walker. The extras, the crew, were all straining to look and Security had to move some barriers to let them pass. The local news reporter and her camera guy dashed away in search of whatever was happening.

J-P hoped that, whoever the ambulances were for, they'd be alright. It required courage, to live. Real effort was needed to exist alongside all the doubt and self-belief and misery, happiness and anger and joy together. He needed just a small part of each; to make his film, to be with Marius, to see him and his dad together.

Life had not been very fair to his dad. *He* had not been very fair to his dad, who was the ghost in his life and not his mum, who was still very present. The truth was that there was anger there, which J-P had buried. He was angry that his mum had died and his dad lived. But he couldn't have ever spoken that anger — it was a terrible thing to admit, even to himself — so he didn't talk to his dad about anything.

He'd ask Maria to call him, as soon as she got back, send a car and get him down on set so he could watch his son working. They can all go for food, afterwards.

He'd love his dad to meet Marius, and Maria. She'll be so pleased when he tells her.

Paul, Aix-en-Provençe — 1890

If he were to count the number of times he has painted this mountain he could go mad, though he never tires of looking at it, never tires of painting it, because, each time, the questions of painting present themselves anew. The questions of colour, the questions of tone and light and shape and form, how to make real the sensations it generates in him.

Mont Saint-Victoire continues to reveal itself, endlessly, but always the work, this mountain, is a new beginning and his own life is caught within it. Still he feels he is seeing its details, complexities, and facets for the first time. He jabs and presses colour into canvas, building, modifying, transforming, making the landscape anew, facing anew the challenges of his life. It is different to him each time because, each time, he is different.

He steps aside from the easel to scrutinise his latest effort, acutely. This mountain is somewhat flat still, a grey, broken triangle (once he has added dark green, white, purple, it will take on depth, assume its truer form), and its surroundings fragmented into a patchwork of green, orange and white (the sky needs more blue to compliment the orange) are placed alongside each other as firmly and instinctively as he is able, today.

Painting demands that you express what you see, not what you think you see. He must have the strength to believe in this, and to act upon it; to be it. "This *is* its truer form," he says. Such statements, the commandments of painting, are easy when directed at a mountain, or an apple, his wife, but more difficult when applied to himself.

He believes intensely, absolutely, in his particular genius, which lies in the ability to express nature, not merely copy it. To express the sensations nature produces upon him everything must be stripped away — the mountain, the trees, the hills, the houses, the sky, even himself — open to receive and convey and express, bypassing conscious reason while using everything he has ever thought, or said, or done, or felt, all at once; stroke by stroke. Many times he fails, while certain in the knowledge only he is capable of occasional success.

How long has he struggled with the purest questions of painting? Too long, and the time has passed so quickly. Is he really different every time he looks at the mountain? Is he so separate from the man he was? "No," he says, as he mixes some purple, certain and uncertain of what he believes, "I am the same as I've ever been." He nods to the mountain. "As are you." And yet, it does look different today.

Today, other thoughts, other works, are encroaching on his endeavours. A new apple painting has imposed itself on his consciousness, involving a pot of primroses, the plant uplifting, containing so many possibilities in its leaves spread wide. Its fragile, delicately assertive flowers refuse to relinquish their grip, even in the face of the mountain, the depths of this landscape.

Today, he can only see the mountain peak as a point of crumpled, stiff white linen piled on a table, the gîtes and farmhouses are his apples, nestled in the folds of a cloth as the buildings are nestled in the folds of the valley, the sky a wall papered in bright blue. The sketched apples, the primroses, call him back to his studio and, try as he might, he cannot resist their pull.

He has always striven to follow his instincts and to dedicate himself obsessively to his painting, because only then can he possibly achieve what lies at his core. He will never compromise that essential truth of himself by creating false drawing now, when his mind is elsewhere.

He will pack up his paints and easel, return to the studio, not allow his frustration at not being able to express the mountain crush him, as it sometimes does, and address those apples instead.

Small parcels of oilcloth are spread out on the ground, and each pocket of living colour, appears now a character in his own life story. His darling son, little Paul, is the vivid cerulean of the sky (he will use this blue against his apples, he decides), Hortense the deep green — often troubling, occasionally soothing — of the trees and woods. His father — black, of course. His mother…? She is the vibrant orange of the ploughed fields and the rooftops. He himself will be the brilliant white that sometimes brings all things together, sometimes creates the spaces between.

Even here, in this open air with all its possibilities of light and colour, even when attempting to express the various sensation of mountain, sky, or trees, (the same heavily-scented pine trees they sheltered under as boys and which give shade next to the very same deep green bodies of water that shimmer invitingly in the late summer afternoons) it is possible to feel trapped inside himself.

"I must paint it *out*."

Crows lift from the field, beat their heavy black wings over his head, as if prompted by him, and an angry buzz, of trapped bees somewhere, fills his ears. The crows are real, the bees are not. They are the sensations he used to paint when he was younger, before he finally settled in his beloved Aix.

He gathers up the parcels of colour into a pile. Émile comes to haunt him, then, in the deep purple he has made to add crucial depth, and substance, and shadow. Try as he might, his present estrangement (there is no other word for it) from the mountain today, has caused fragments of his friend to persist in a piercing sensation, like a knife being plunged in his belly.

How could someone who loved him so well get him so wrong? How well can he himself be the judge of that? Does he even care to know himself — what is that compared to his art? Such questions are harder, even, than the questions of painting.

Happiness is not a state that has been much ascribed to him, though some of his paintings are so happy he hears them singing as he brings them into being. He has never admitted this to anyone, has achieved a deep contentment in his struggle, in the idea of struggle and doubt, brought on by the acceptance that it is the best state for him to work, if not to live.

Painting Hortense had been different, though the portraits had a habit of breaking apart, or the impetus for them dissolved. They made each other anxious — she because he demanded her full attention, though he was hardly aware of this much of the time, or when his frustration erupted into fury because he could only see her as a complex relation of shapes and colours (her oval face still pleasing), and certainly no longer as the woman he had known when they began their courtship.

By killing off, at the end of his book, his failed and despairing version of him, Émile had joined in with the bullies they'd always fought against. First as boys when they would have died for each other, it seemed, and then as young men at the Salon and the École, and against his father's attempts to control and stifle through all of that. He still aches with the injury of that betrayal. Held up to ridicule, exposed like an apple's insides that brown and wizen in air.

What unnerves and agitates him now, what will drive him back to his studio today, is the unhappy but sincere sensation that there was truth in Émile's written portrait of him. Perhaps their friendship could have survived, but it was not he who struck the mortal blow.

The mountain, as he straightens up and looks at it, calms him. He straps the canvas to his back, folds up his easel and tucks it under his arm, and makes off down the path towards home. His life has come full circle; there are local boys who follow him through the countryside even now, laughing and throwing things, as has happened always. But, now, he faces these trials alone.

How much harder it is to retain your ideals in the face of scorn, mockery and abject failure. Even the impetus one gains from that as a young man soon fades. The fight is exhausting when it is relentless.

Is his life's work to go unrecognised? Did Émile truly believe it was Paul's destiny to be the painter who creates revolution in others but whose genius is unappreciated? He could resign himself to this fate, as others who have changed the way the world sees itself must resign themselves.

He may not shatter the Louvre, as he and Émile had once dreamed, but he can keep his vow to astonish Paris with an apple. Even if he paints a hundred failures it will all be worth it for that one moment. He cares nothing now for acceptance, for posterity — he doesn't care about the past or the future, only the present, what he is thinking about now — the apples, the primroses, the tablecloth, the landscape, the mountain, the houses, the sky, Hortense, little Paul, Émile, his mother and father, himself, all mixed together.

He stops on the path and turns to regard the mountain once more before he loses sight of it. It is through his painting that he begins — still only begins — to understand who he is, and that is as constant and never-ending a struggle as solving the problem of painting.

He most belongs in the eternal present, addressing the questions of painting, of life, moment by moment, as they arise.

Jeffrey, Hong Kong — 2013

Yo Yo shuffles from one side of the screen to the other. She does not have the painting with her, as they had arranged. Jeffrey can only assume that she has either failed him, or betrayed him. He'll make her wait.

He had sprung into action as soon as his father's plan revealed itself to him. All the signs had been there and he had only to open himself up to see. He'd monitored the painting machine recreating *Still Life with Apples and Jug* including on those days when its mechanical arms dangled idly, the unfinished canvas waiting, biding its time. Jeffrey figured the machine was programmed to mimic the estimated timeframe of Cézanne's original production, and in four weeks it was done.

Walter had clung on for almost three months, until yesterday. His determination to deprive Jeffrey of the only thing he cared to inherit surely his main motive for living. How foolish Jeffrey had been to think his father might change as he approached the end. Walter Yeung was toying with him, with his mother's memory, with the whole fucking world. Well, Jeffrey wouldn't let him win.

But he knew he couldn't do this alone. He'd considered involving the doctor in his scheme, but this prospect concerned him; either the doctor would have informed Walter, and so ruined everything, or he would have agreed to Jeffrey's plan, accepted his bribe, and thereby destroy Jeffrey's image of him. He's not sure which would have been worse.

Gordon Li, having already proven himself open to corruption, was not the person Jeffrey could entrust to handle his mother's beloved painting. That had left him with one remaining option. When he'd summoned Yo Yo she came immediately.

She'd claimed curiosity as her main motivation, and he had laughed openly at her. "Nothing to do with money then?"

"I don't need your money," she'd flashed back at him. "I am Walter Yeung's personal assistant, remember?"

She'd spun on her heels to go and Jeffrey heard himself bark at her, "Yo Yo, stay!" in the voice of his father and, disgusted at himself, adopted a gentler tone. "He's not going to be here forever, Yo Yo. Please," he said, "if you help me, I will make sure that your own family will be well taken care of. I know you have a sick father of your own, three younger sisters to support, and elderly grandparents. You are well paid, but not that well. Let me help them, if not you."

Yo Yo had turned back to Jeffrey, and waited for him to speak.

Eventually, he did, pacing the room. "All this time, even as he's dying, he's trying to take my mother's memory away from me. To keep her for himself by — by bribing her with the gift he knows she would most appreciate."

Jeffrey became increasingly frantic.

"He must be stopped. It would be a terrible violation of my mother's love and of her love — her love for the painting." He'd slumped down on his bed, then, struggling to breathe.

Yo Yo had poured a glass of water and, as she handed it to him, he caught the dizzying scent of flowers drifting from her hair. He had to make her understand. "To allow my father to lock away the painting, to let it rot alongside him in his grave — that would be a form of *murder*. I won't be his accomplice. Please, Yo Yo."

He gestured towards the chair at his desk and she perched on its edge, settling herself.

"What do you propose?" she asked, tentatively.

He had her. "We have to rescue it. You will be an essential part of the plan, Yo Yo. I — I need you. Gordon Li is in my pay." He waited for her look of surprise to dissipate. "He has agreed to engineer a power outage that will shut down our security systems and keep them out of operation for half an hour. He doesn't know the reason for my request and I would prefer to keep it that way. We will — *you* will — have that short amount of time before the system reboots. The real painting must be swapped for its replica, or else be lost."

Yo Yo remained silent, regarding him impassively.

Jeffrey jumped up, spilling his water across the floor. "Surely you can see, Yo Yo — you have to help me. You *have* to. Please…"

"I do understand, and I will help you, Master Yeung. However, you must understand that I undertake this task not out of disloyalty to your father, nor out of respect for your mother — I am sorry, but I do not care about her memory, and I do not care about you. As for my own family, I have all the money we will ever need. Walter has promised me that himself. I will do this for the painting, and the painting alone. It's too beautiful to come to such an end."

Jeffrey had been stunned by this speech. He had watched her so often, and didn't know her mind, her voice, at all before then. He only hoped he could direct her long enough for her to do what he needed. "I am grateful," he said, "thank you."

Their plan was simple. Just the day before — his father's final day

— he had sent his coded message to Gordon Li and, within seconds, the screens had gone blank. Everything was in darkness.

Powerless, and not knowing what else to do with himself, Jeffrey had played out the scheme in his mind's eye. He'd picked up his joystick and used it to direct Yo Yo stealthily through the entrance of Walter's suite, along the corridor, into his sitting room as the clock ticked down the thirty minutes allotted to her. Would she make a noise? Give herself away? No. Jeffrey had pressed the red button on his joystick and, in his imagination, she'd made the switch easily. After that, the cameras and the screens had all blinked back to life as suddenly as they'd gone dark. There was the painting on the wall, seemingly undisturbed, though there was no way of yet knowing whether Yo Yo had succeeded.

Then, Jeffrey had turned his attention to his father's bedroom only to freeze at the sight of the doctor unfolding the white cotton square he'd taken from his suit jacket pocket, and covering Walter's face with it. He had missed the moment of his father's death and he didn't know what that even meant to him.

The doctor and Walter's lawyer had performed their subsequent duties diligently and swiftly. Walter's money and power had ensured there would be no need for an autopsy. The doctor wheeled in the coffin on its gurney, and Jeffrey watched as he carefully, respectfully, lifted the body into it. Even shrouded by the sheet Jeffrey could see how emaciated Walter had become, the doctor exerting himself no more than he would by picking up his briefcase. He'd dismissed the lawyer before pushing the open coffin into the sitting room. Then, Jeffrey watched as the doctor had taken Cézanne's *Still Life with Apples and Jug* from the wall and laid it face down on top of Walter's body, before closing the coffin lid.

Unable to sleep, he has been watching China Central Television. His father's death was announced quickly, along with a declaration from the Board of CantoCorp of business as usual. All this was necessary to end the uncertainty, the kind that shareholders, stock markets and governments fear.

Tributes had immediately been paid to the man who had been such an inspiration to so many, an asset to the People's Republic and the engine of its economy.

"Walter Yeung will be afforded the rare honour," the CCTV anchor woman had intoned, "of a lying in state, before he is laid to rest beside his wife and baby son who died so tragically over twenty years ago."

They had showed a thirty-minute special: *Walter Yeung — Man of the People* — that told, in breathless, unflinching reconstruction, the cobbled-together story behind the 'most important' episodes of Walter's life, including, of course, the most important episode of Jeffrey's life.

Jeffrey watched, despite himself, as his mother's car was swept off the road and tumbled down the ridge in slow motion, a screaming mouth superimposed over the dramatic scene. To an accompaniment of swirling strings, a torrent of CGI flowers burst out of the container lorry, down, down, down, covering the upturned car.

Finally, over the soft-focus image of a baby lying on a bed of pink blossom, haloed by the flowers, the voiceover speculated on the whereabouts of Walter Yeung's surviving son, Jeffrey, not seen for many years: "It is to this already fortunate young man that Walter Yeung has bequeathed his business, his fortune, his spectacular art collection. What now," the commentator asked, "for the future of CantoCorp and all those whose livelihoods depend on it?"

They'd interviewed people in the street, just as they had after Gor Gor's death. Each of them described Walter as a 'great man', a 'true hero', as someone who inspired them to work hard and achieve their dreams of wealth and material things.

The reporter then asked one of a group of young women if she had a message for the 'mysterious Jeffrey Yeung'. She paused before looking directly into the camera: "Will you marry me?" she'd said, and her friends erupted into giggles.

Now, he presses his keyboard and the door to his suite slides open. Yo Yo enters and he keeps his back to her, takes a deep, deep breath and says, "So. Tell me."

Yo Yo's reply comes quiet and steady. "Everything went as planned."

Jeffrey spins round in his chair. "Then where is it? The real Cézanne? You were supposed to bring it to me. That was our arrangement." Jeffrey tries to hold himself in but his exasperation spills over. "You *do* want more money," he spits, "is that it?"

"I told you," Yo Yo snaps, "exactly why I agreed to this. Money has nothing to do with it. I went to fetch the painting, as I said I would. I took hold of the frame" — she brings her hands up, reconstructing the scene Jeffrey had already envisioned — "and the canvas shone, filling my field of vision. It — it *spoke* to me."

"It — spoke?"

"I know it sounds strange — but these are emotional times for all of us. It told me that, if I brought the painting here, it would be as good as buried — sealed in the living tomb you've made for yourself. That too would be a — a *murder* — wasn't that how you described it?"

"You would never speak to my father in this way," Jeffrey shouts. "If he were here — "

"He is not here," Yo Yo interjects.

She puts a hand to her face and Jeffrey recognises the gesture from when Walter struck her on his birthday, as if the memory has made itself physically present. This is her revenge for that and all his other slights,

Jeffrey thinks. She is defying him now. "Yo Yo," he whispers, urgently, "I know you hated my father too. You must understand how I feel?"

"No. I felt sorry for him. And for you. Fools, both of you. Utter fools."

It's as if his mother's chastising voice echoes through her, transmitted through time. It is unbearable.

"You are just like him," Yo Yo continues. "The great Walter Yeung only ever wanted one thing — the love of his remaining son — and you denied him that. You could have had everything and you threw it all away to stay in this — this luxurious *pit* — and become the Lone Wolf."

Jeffrey gazes in astonishment on hearing her say his other, secret name.

"How could you think we didn't know, Jeffrey? Did you really suppose you could do all that without Walter Yeung's knowledge, without his permission? He *knew*. He knew the whole time. And he was proud of your work. Proud of you…"

"Did he — did he say that?"

"No, but I saw. When one of your works appeared on his computer he feigned indifference, but I saw him return time and time again to the flowers you were sending to the world."

"And still he never spoke to me?"

"I saw," — Yo Yo continues, as if Jeffrey has said nothing, has not leaped from the bed, is not now towering above her — "I saw the truth that lay beneath his silence."

"And what truth was that?"

"Pain." Yo Yo groaned the word. "And flowers. Do you realise how difficult that was for him? I will never understand your cruelty — that you would want to remind him, and the entire world, of that great tragedy that ruined your lives. Oh, good for you Jeffrey Yeung. Bravo! You made sure that he could never speak to you. You created an insurmountable firewall of flowers, over and over again."

223

Jeffrey backs away now.

Yo Yo puts on a mimicking whine: "*And still he never spoke to me.* Well, I don't blame him. How could he articulate a combination of such pride and deep sorrow? What words are there for that? He thought your whole life's work was an effort to punish him for something for which he was not responsible. And all this time you were ignorant, each of you was ignorant of the other's despair."

Jeffrey collapses onto his bed, drained of all energy, curls up, unable to speak. She will not bring the painting to him. That's her revenge for all that's passed. It will be lost forever, and so his mother is lost, finally, irrevocably.

Yo Yo kneels next to him, speaks softly. "This is what happens when you lock yourself away aged fifteen. You remain an angry child."

He glares at her, eyes stinging with tears.

"I'm sorry," she murmurs, "but if you want the painting you must retrieve it yourself."

With that, she withdraws to the doorway.

The impossibility of what she proposes shocks Jeffrey back into voice. "What? No. No, I can't do that!"

Yo Yo nods firmly. "Yes. You must."

Jeffrey shakes his head and Yo Yo offers him an outstretched hand. "I'll help you. I will help you through."

So, not revenge. Instead, a kind of test. Somehow he knows he can do it. He takes her hand, small and pale, her fingernails bitten right down. It is the first he has held for too many years. He pulls himself up.

"You must open the door," Yo Yo tells him.

Jeffrey turns towards his keyboard but she stops him. "No, not like that. Say it. Say the word."

Jeffrey croaks into the air: "Open."

Nothing happens.

"Again," Yo Yo says.

He clears his throat and uses his father's bark, "Open," and the door slides back.

They walk out into the corridor and it is so, so easy.

Yo Yo lets go of his hand and he floats through the space, dizzy for a moment as if tumbling down a ridge, and he can smell flowers, but that's impossible. Then he recalls the floral scent from Yo Yo's hair. Did Walter smell it too, all that time she worked for him? Did she wear it deliberately — her own act of cruelty?

"You know the way from here," she says.

Yes, Jeffrey does know.

Cameras turn to follow his progress down the corridor, though no one will be watching. CantoCorp headquarters has been closed as a mark of respect — today, it is a crystal mausoleum.

Jeffrey calls the elevator, steps inside, alone, pushes the illuminated B and counts the thirty two seconds, his lips moving as his father's used to do.

When the elevator comes to a halt, Jeffrey hesitates. Stepping out of its warm, protective cubicle is proving inexplicably harder than stepping out of his room. It means crossing into his father's domain. But he remembers his vision and his quest to retrieve the painting and mustn't fail. He pushes through his fear, can almost feel the gilt wood frame in his hands. Soon it will hang in his own rooms.

He strides purposefully to the door, punches in the security code — the date of his and Walter Junior's birthday — and enters his father's suite.

It is even worse than he imagined. The ceilings are low, spot lit, the maroon carpets deathly thick, the dark wooden panelling heavy and oppressive. The country-house hotel look he had seen on the screen looks even more like a cheap film set in reality. Taking a gulp of air, Jeffrey plunges towards the sitting room and through the door.

Automatic lights flicker on, immediately.

The cameras, alerted by his movement, bleep and whirr to face him.

He lets out a cry of alarm when he sees Walter Yeung, his father, is standing right there.

Jeffrey's stomach heaves and he struggles to breathe as his legs give way beneath him. Suddenly an arm is round his back, another under his legs, and he is borne up like a child, placed into a chair.

His bleary eyes come into focus and he sees it's not his father at all, but the doctor. It was the doctor who carried him, setting him down in a gentle recline with the same tender care he'd shown Walter's corpse.

"I — " Jeffrey gasps " — what are you doing here?"

"I've been waiting for you." The doctor's voice is deep and soft, just as he thought.

"For me? How did you know I would come?"

"I didn't, not for certain. But I am following orders from someone who did."

"Yo Yo." A flash of cold fear passes through him — fear that he really has been betrayed after all. Who can he trust? He will never get what he's come for. "That little witch has told you everything?"

"Master Yeung, calm yourself, please." The doctor kneels next to him, lifts Jeffrey's wrist to check his pulse. He is wearing, not his customary sharp black suit, but Walter's dove grey tailored wool and oyster-coloured silk necktie. And are those really the doctor's fingers, with small dark hairs on his knuckles, nails carefully trimmed and buffed, gripping Jeffrey's wrist? He smells… he smells of lemon, with black pepper, is that it? Then it comes to him. It's hair oil, the same brand as his father's, a scent Jeffrey didn't even know he remembered.

Jeffrey suddenly starts. He is sitting in Walter's chair. So then where — where is the painting?

As if reading his thoughts, the doctor moves to one side and reveals Cézanne's *Still Life with Apples and Jug* hanging on the wall directly in front of him.

It's smaller than he envisioned, that's his first impression. Those funny-looking apples. The wonky table. His mind a blank, he can't now remember his mother's words about it, why she'd loved it. He's no better than his father. "Is this it?" Jeffrey asks. "The real one?"

"This is it," the doctor affirms. "The real one."

Jeffrey feels… nothing. Empty. He looks, for the first time, into the doctor's extraordinary eyes, one dark brown, almost black, the other a lighter green, flecked with amber. How many points of interest such as this have passed Jeffrey by, completely unnoticed, on those bleeping, monochrome, fuzzy screens? He feels nothing for the doctor either, no desire, that is, standing next to him in his tired-looking three-dimensional state, the man whose imagined touch Jeffrey has fantasised about for some time. What to say about the painting or the man?

Jeffrey starts with a simple statement of fact. He says, "She loved this painting."

"So your father told me."

"Did I do the right thing by preventing it from being buried with him?"

"What do you think your mother would have wanted?"

"Oh, she would have wanted it to carry on living in this world, I'm certain."

"So there is your answer. It's what your mother would have wanted. And your father, too."

"No." Jeffrey says. "You know full well what his wishes were."

"I do. After all, I am here with you now because I'm following Walter Yeung's wishes."

"His? I don't — "

"He felt you should have someone you could trust with you when you finally came to collect it. After all these years of mutual silence, he still knew you better than anyone." The doctor speaks as if giving Jeffrey a diagnosis. "Your father knew what you'd do when you saw the painting being copied. That's why he did it. He knew it was the only way to get you out."

Jeffrey could laugh, really, just laugh. Even in death Walter was playing games, but he didn't hate him any longer. He had no energy for it. He didn't know what he felt. "I should have told him," he whispers. "I should have told him everything I felt about my mother, and my brother, about Gor Gor, my work, about me — I should have told him…"

"You were not wrong in your assessment of your father. I know what kind of a man he was. He instructed me to wear his clothes when you entered — my costume fooling you into seeing him for a moment, just as it did. He wanted to shock you into life — no, that's not the word he used — he wanted to *astonish* you into life. That was it. I didn't approve, but I agreed because he was like a father to me…"

The doctor slumps down on the footstool, succumbing to exhaustion. He, too, must not have slept much these recent nights, Jeffrey realises, what with all the waiting; not just for Walter's demise, but knowing it would necessitate the part he was having to play now — explaining the outcome of the game.

"He was?" Jeffrey asks. He could not have foreseen any of this.

"Pardon me," the doctor says. "I understand that's an impertinence, but it's the truth. My own father worked on a CantoCorp construction site and, one day, Walter overheard him and a colleague talking about future hopes for their children. My interest in medicine was likely to lead to nothing because my parents didn't have the money to send me away to study. The very next day your father sent my father a cheque. Near the end of my first year at medical school my father died — lung cancer — and I thought I would have to leave my career behind, find a job and help my mother, but Walter continued to pay my father's salary to her. Then, after I graduated, I became his only doctor. I really owe him everything."

His father really had come to understand the possibilities of looking in his last months. Walter and Jeffrey had really seen inside each other, this whole past decade, even though they never spoke.

And Walter had done this vital thing for Jeffrey — freed him from his grief and astonished him back into the world, as he intended. Ultimately, it was not the painting that had brought him here, it was his father. He really was an extraordinary man. Walter's true gift to Annie, his wife and the mother of his children, in the afterlife, their life yet to come, would be Jeffrey's life.

He realises he is crying and the doctor takes a cotton handkerchief — identical to the one he had laid over Walter's face — from his pocket and hands it to Jeffrey.

Jeffrey covers his own face with it, dries his eyes. The handkerchief carries a light cologne, the reviving scent of tobacco flowers. Walter had denied this pleasure in his lifetime's state of grief, and Jeffrey yearns, now, to see him again, to press his hand against his father's hand, even though Walter will never know. Maybe that could be arranged, if it's not too late.

"Given what you have just told me," Jeffrey says, "we are practically brothers." This is the truth of it. As well as leaving him the painting, and freeing him, Jeffrey's father has bequeathed him a new connection to the past — an older brother. "What's your first name? I don't know it."

"Shen. My name is Shen."

"I'm going to need your help, Shen. All the arrangements are in place, I know. Apparently, Hong Kong is about to witness the biggest funeral it has seen since — well, since Leslie Cheung's. And a museum opening too, on the same day. Can you imagine? Could you — will you go with me?"

"Of course, Jeffrey. I wouldn't want to miss it."

Jeffrey stands up and approaches the painting. "This is the real one? No more surprises?"

The doctor laughs — something Jeffrey has really never heard before. "No, no more surprises." It really is a warm, gentle voice.

"You strange thing," Jeffrey says, examining the layers of red and green and brown and purple, all built up by one man. Unexpected colours shimmer in his sight as if after a long period of blindness. He steps back to take in its depth and texture. The surface vibrates, like a living thing. He considers his own creations, his digital versions of dim memories of flowers. Flowers and memories made of numbers and code.

"How do you begin to paint an apple, a tablecloth, or a mountain?"

He asks this aloud, not to Shen who has come to stand beside him, but to the painting, into the air.

You put down one stroke of paint, he thinks, and then another, and then another, and, after a pause, perhaps, another, until you have it. Until you've put down colour, light, shadow, and the spaces in between.

Jeffrey will undertake a new project, yes, a biopic of sorts, about his father: *A Portrait of Walter Yeung*. And it will be a true portrait — there's no real value in anything else — of the complicated, difficult, terrible and brilliant man he was.

He hopes he can persuade Yo Yo to stay and work for him. If she agrees — and he truly hopes she will — her first task will be to contact J-P McKeown, ask if he would consider a collaboration.

He'll invite Sophie Greene, too. Bring her and her daughter to Hong Kong. He thinks they might have valuable work to make together, or, if not, she would no doubt like to be away from New York and her ex for a while. Yes, if she wants it, he can do this for her.

He'll make a new work of art, one that will shine a light on his and Walter's fractious relationship, exploring the rift that came to exist between father and son, the grief-made gap that neither of them knew how to bridge.

Perhaps too, Jeffrey can play a game of his own, combining the footage he has amassed, watching Walter from an intimate distance, with an unflinching portrayal of himself.

At the very end, only as the credits roll, he will reveal his secret identity as the Lone Wolf to the rest of the world. What a triumphant surprise that will be!

He's sure his father would love that. It will be Jeffrey's gift to him.

Acknowledgements

It's been a long and winding road to get to this point and I have had a lot of help along the way.

Huge thanks to my agent, editor, and chief supporter, Laura Macdougall, and everyone else at United Agents. Also, #TeamMacdougall are a wonderful group of lovely people and I feel extremely fortunate to be a member of this writers' community.

Thanks to all at Lume Books for believing in me and putting my work out into the world. Bless you, James Nunn, for the stunning cover artwork. Your particular tribute to Cézanne is better than I could have imagined.

I've had feedback, encouragement, and invaluable advice from Esther Freud, Cherry Smyth, Jenni Fagan, Swithun Cooper, Jo Minogue, Mariana Villas Boas, Colin Ginks, and Rob Plews. I'm grateful to everyone.

My family, friends, and extended family have been a constant bedrock and safety net throughout my whole life and I'm very lucky to have them all.

Special gratitude is due to my husband, Henrique Neves Lopes, whose love gets me up in the morning and helps me sleep at night. *Todo o meu amor, sempre*. You have me heart and soul.